WHEN ANGELS PLAY POKER

Maura O'Leary

Inspiring Voices

Inspiring Voices books may be ordered through booksellers or by contacting:

Inspiring Voices
1663 Liberty Drive
Bloomington, IN 47403
www.inspiringvoices.com
1 (866) 697-5313

ISBN: 978-1-4624-1213-6 (sc)
ISBN: 978-1-4624-1214-3 (hc)
ISBN: 978-1-4624-1212-9 (e)

Library of Congress Control Number: 2017904351

Scripture taken from the King James Version of the Bible.

Print information available on the last page.

Inspiring Voices rev. date: 04/25/2017

To my beloved Babbo

CHAPTER 1

Last Thoughts

Jimmy practically skipped down the hallway of the retirement complex to his room. He would have literally skipped, but he was sixty-four and didn't want his babe of the night, who was watching him, to see his attempt at skipping especially if it came across as lame. Instead he tried to look and *be* cool. It was his MO in life. *Why change now?*

Man, oh man, he thought as he entered his room and quickly shut the door. He looked around his tiny apartment and realized he had just made what was by far his best con move. Though he was a seasoned con man, he had to admit it was pure luck—and some masterful BS—that had gotten him into and accepted at the town's best retirement home.

He mused, *No harm in lying a bit about age, disability, and joblessness, and throwing in a bit of luck as well!*

And lucky is what I'm gonna get tonight. Yeah! Jimmy smiled and clapped his hands. *Who knew that a retirement home would actually have some good-looking chicks' right down the hall?*

To top it all off, even his brother Bob was stunned that he'd gotten into the place. Bob wanted to celebrate by taking Jimmy furniture shopping the next day. Thinking of Bob made Jimmy remember the message he'd left him earlier that day, razzing him about having a good time with his girl that night and wanting all the juicy details when they met.

Jimmy jumped in the shower, and as he was lathering up, he mused, *How ironic! We're both lucky men tonight! Bob won't be the only one with a story.*

As Jimmy came out of shower and started to get dressed, his thoughts wandered to Bob's girlfriend. *She must be pretty amazing, because I've never seen my brother so happy. I hope I get to meet her soon. She sounds like my kind of woman—lots of curves, Irish, and feisty. Who knows? Maybe if Bob messes this up, I'll have a go at her and repair the damage.*

This made Jimmy smile and then shake his head quickly. He had other things to think about.

Now smartly dressed in a nice blue shirt, blue jeans, and leather jacket, Jimmy walked over to the dresser, looked in the mirror, and murmured, "Forget Bob's girl. I have my own hot woman to think about and get back to"

He reached across the dresser to his favorite cologne and suddenly felt an excruciating pain go up his right arm. Jimmy tried to move it a certain way to ease the pain, but instead the cologne fell out of his hand, crashing to the floor.

And Jimmy followed it.

The last thing he remembered thinking, as he hit the floor, was *I'm not going to get lucky tonight.* And then everything went black.

CHAPTER 2

"Hey, You're in Heaven Now!"

Jimmy woke up to the brightest light he had ever seen, and it was surrounding him in every direction he looked. It had a feeling of warmth to it, like the sun, which made him wish desperately for some shades. He reached instinctively into his pocket and realized he was touching air. And when he looked down, all he saw was a white formation—and no clothes. This had him a bit panicky and confused, but also annoyed.

He shouted, "Where the hell are my sunglasses? Damn it! And better yet, where the hell am I?"

He suddenly noticed that he was in a white hallway, and a little old man was zooming down the hall toward him, like he was on some mobile scooter. But from what Jimmy could see, there was no scooter. He was moving toward him at a good clip, and the man had a *big* file under his arm. As Jimmy stared at him, transfixed, he realized that the man was sort of gliding along, but with a mission.

The man finally stopped right in front of Jimmy, who towered over him, looked up, and said, "Hello, Jimmy. I'm Master Norman. I am your elder guide. In answer to your outburst of questions, let me tell you something you must never forget: Do *not* say *hell* here! It's not allowed."

Jimmy looked down at him and said, "Hey there, little man, I really don't care if you don't like my language. I am a bit peeved at the moment because I've got a really hot chick waiting for me. I plan on getting laid tonight, and for some crazy reason, I seem to have hit a major detour down a white hallway with you."

Norm burst out laughing. "You could definitely say you've hit a detour, my friend. A somewhat permanent one, I might add. Just be glad it's a white hallway instead of a dark one."

"Well," Jimmy said, "quite frankly, the brightness is really getting to me. Do you have some shades I can borrow?"

"We don't need shades up here, Jimmy," Norm patiently said. "We welcome the light, and so must you. You'll adjust quicker to the brightness that way."

"You still haven't answered my question," Jimmy said impatiently. "Where the hell am I!"

"Well, Jimmy, exactly the opposite. You are not anywhere near hell. You are in heaven now."

"What?" Jimmy shouted in disbelief. "Look, little zoom meister with the big file in hand, you seem a bit out there. I am *not* in heaven. I was just leaving my room, ready to walk a corridor, which wasn't all white, to meet up with a hot babe. Furthermore, I don't even know how you know me."

Norm fidgeted a bit with the file in his arms and said, "Yes, well, umm, we're all very aware of what your intentions were tonight, *but* your time was up. And it was decided, by the highest power, to end things before your, umm, little escapade."

Jimmy had started pacing in the corridor. He whirled around and said, "You've got to be BS'ing me. I am *not* in heaven. I feel great! I mean, look at me. I'm walking and talking and could even be chewing gum at the same time, if I had some."

Norm sighed and said, "Jimmy, I know it's hard to believe, but you're no longer in your body. If you don't believe me, go ahead and touch your arm."

"Alrighty then, I'll show you." He reached out for his arm and—as when he had reached for his sunglasses—all he felt was air. Jimmy's eyes widened when he realized he couldn't feel anything. He looked at Norm and could see a smug look of "I told you so" on his face.

Jimmy started walking backward, yelling at Norm, "Hey, you, what type of sick trick is this? Get away from me! I can't feel anything, anywhere! What did you do to me? Wait a second. I know what this is. You've abducted me and taken me to Mars, haven't you?"

Norm chuckled and said, "Noooo, Jimmy, you are not on Mars. You're in heaven, as I told you. And quite frankly, if I were you, I'd pipe down about it. You're very lucky to be here."

Jimmy studied Norm seriously for a moment and could see that the weird little old man wasn't joking. He quickly asked in a quieter tone, "What does that mean?"

"It means that the huge file I've been lugging around, which is almost as big as I am, is your life history. Good deeds versus bad deeds are all marked down in the file. And unfortunately for you, because you were a con artist, there is a lot of bad versus good in here."

"Hey now! Whoa! Wait a minute. I think you should peruse slowly back through that huge file and focus on my wonderful childhood," Jimmy said in a huff. "That shall quickly even out the good, the bad, and the ugly. I definitely belong on the good side for everything I went through early in life." He was definitely unnerved to find out that, like Santa Claus, people in heaven kept a good and a bad list. *Damn, no one told me that one!*

Norm could see that Jimmy was getting agitated, so he calmly said, "We already did that, Jimmy—took your childhood into serious consideration. And that is *why* you are here."

"Well, that's just terrific, little man! Let's all celebrate. Open bar for everyone!" Jimmy said sarcastically.

"Jimmy, we don't drink in heaven." Norm stated seriously.

"Oh, that's great. This place is just getting better and better by the moment." Jimmy retorted.

By this point, Norm could see that Jimmy was getting more wired by the minute. In addition, he knew that, like most people who had just arrived in heaven, Jimmy was feeling confused and displaced. Norm decided to bring in the reunion gang. This was always one of the best parts of his job. It never failed to move him.

Meanwhile, Jimmy had spotted a door down the corridor a few feet away. "Hey, Norm, what's behind the big white door?"

"Behind that door is the end of your journey, Jimmy, and the beginning of eternal life."

"Hang on a second! Where are the Pearly Gates? Did I not make the invite list? Because of my bad deeds, am I being sent through the back door? Wow! Wouldn't the religious zealots back on earth love to know this one *big* news flash: 'People, there are two doors, not one.'" By this point, he was stomping back and forth in the hallway.

"Hey there, Jimmy, calm down! You did go through the Pearly Gates, but unfortunately you weren't awake for the visual."

"Okay," Jimmy said firmly. "Here's the deal, Norm. I'll walk through this door up ahead, *but* if anything looks suspicious or shady, I am *out of here!*"

"Really, Jimmy?" said Norm calmly. "Well, there is nowhere else to go—except down, of course—so go to hell if you want."

Jimmy rolled his eyes, and said, "We'll see about that. Just open the door."

Norm did that with a grand gesture and then stepped back to watch the spectacle. There was nothing like watching what happened next; it truly was his most favorite moment every time.

Jimmy turned and stared in disbelief at what he saw in front of him. The first person there when the door opened was his sister, Pat, who had died several years before from cancer. She stood there smiling, and he was instantly surrounded by a very warm and bright light. He could feel total love and joy emanating from her. The feeling was so powerful, it overwhelmed him.

Jimmy didn't know what to say. He didn't want the moment to ever end. His sister looked radiant, the most beautiful he ever remembered her looking on earth, and she seemed very happy. He realized it was worth it to die, if only to see her.

Then he looked beyond her and saw other people, ones he had not seen in decades in some cases: war buddies, kids he grew up with, and some distant relatives. It was unbelievable to him.

All of a sudden, Jimmy felt like he was talking to them all at once. Then he realized that, yes, he was doing that, but not really talking. It was all done by telepathy, which he realized was much faster than talking. Yet his emotions were still there, and he could convey them easily. He can also feel their emotions— joy, love, surprise-based on the level of warmth coming from them to him. All of this was happening instantly around him.

It was the coolest thing Jimmy had ever experienced. It was overwhelming, but in a wonderful way. All of those people who had made him the happiest in life were surrounding him in death. This revelation made Jimmy realize that he was lucky to be there. It was awesome to know that he would be able to hang out with his sister and friends endlessly in the future. He thought, *now THAT is cool.*

He turned, looked at Norm, and said, "Thank you, Norm, for bringing me to see the people I loved the most when they were on earth. I'm sorry if I gave you such a hard time earlier, cause if this *IS* heaven, that's just fine with me!" he grinned.

Norman bowed and said, "Well, Jimmy, we're all so glad you approve. I'll give you another few minutes to visit with them, and then we need to move on."

Jimmy stared at Norm in disbelief. "Wait! What do you mean I have a few minutes left to visit with them? I want to hang with my sister and friends that I haven't seen in years. I want to stay with them."

"Jimmy, I know this is hard, but unfortunately we need to continue moving along."

"Oh yeah? Well, where are we going that's so important I have to cut short visiting my sister, who I've missed a great deal? We have a lot to catch up on."

Norm replied, "You'll see soon enough. But one important piece is that you'll be given an important assignment. Now don't waste any more time asking me questions!"

Jimmy turned around and went back to the warmer light around his sister. He realized that she had the brightest light of anyone around him, so he asked, "Why is your light so bright?"

Pat replied, "Because I'm an angel, Jimmy, at a higher power level than you and everyone else here."

"Wow, that's so cool! Leave it to my sis to be at the top of the class, even in heaven," Jimmy laughed. "Can I be like you?"

She replied with a soft smile, "Not yet, Jimmy. It takes a long time."

With that, they started exchanging telepathic thoughts at the same time eagerly, and Pat accelerated the thought speed because she wanted to find out everything she could about what had happened over the last several years on earth while Jimmy and she had been apart.

Before Jimmy knew it, Norman was signaling to him that he needed to leave and move on. Jimmy turned back to his sister and said, "When and how can I see you again?"

Pat sighed and said, "It probably won't be for a while, Jimmy. But don't worry, as soon as you complete your assignment, you'll be allowed to hang with me for a bit."

Jimmy looked discouraged. "Pat, this just isn't fair! I thought when you went to heaven you got to hang out with your loved ones, and protect those on earth you left behind as well. I thought I could hang with you, and we'd watch over the funeral together. Speaking of the funeral, how is everyone handling my death? How did I die? I don't even know that much!"

Pat said solemnly, "Unfortunately, badly. Your heart attack was so sudden, everyone is in shock, even your ex-wives. But the people who are taking it the hardest are Mom and Bobby."

Jimmy started to pace again. He turned to Norm and said, "Damn it, I need to be there! I need to be watching over my brother, mom, kids, and others. That better be my assignment, Norm."

Pat said quickly, "Jimmy, don't worry. I'm watching over the family, and I will be at the funeral."

Jimmy looked at her solemnly and said, "Okay, I feel better knowing that. But promise me you'll check in, especially on Bobby. He gets depressed sometimes, and this is gonna send him reeling."

Pat smiled and said, "Never worry about that. I watch over Bob every day." With that she turned and in a blink of an eye was gone.

Norm had Jimmy slowly walk away after saying good-bye

to his remaining friends. Then the two of them started to glide away at a slow pace in the opposite direction. Jimmy looked back sadly at them and then turned forward and concentrated on gliding along in heaven, thinking, *"What a wild and crazy day this has been"*.

CHAPTER 3

The Assignment

As Norm and Jimmy slowly glided along, Norm commented, "We'll go to a meeting chamber to discuss where we go from here and what your assignment will be, Jimmy."

They continued until they came to an alcove, which they entered and immediately saw in front of them a beautiful, lush green courtyard with a waterfall cascading over a beautiful rock garden. Jimmy had never seen such a sight in his life. He was awestruck by the waterfall.

They sat down on a bench in the garden, and Norm opened the big, thick file he had been lugging around with him since Jimmy had set eyes upon him. He poured through a couple of front pages, looked up at Jimmy, and said, "You're now a Level 1 guardian angel, Jimmy, otherwise known as a spirit guide. And that's where you'll be staying for a while until you get a few successful assignments under your belt."

Jimmy pondered this for a minute and asked, "What level is my sister?"

"She's a Level 8 angel."

"Geez, I guess I won't be hanging with her anytime soon!" Jimmy said with a discouraged grimace.

Norm gently said, "For now that is true, but if it makes you feel any better, the person you'll be assigned to is a former Level 8 angel."

"Huh?" said Jimmy, looking tired and confused.

"The person we're assigning you, luckily for you, is a very old soul. That's why she was a Level 8. But sadly she's being strongly tested in her latest visit to earth, and we're concerned that she might come back unworthy of being a Level 8, based on her future actions on earth." Norm sighed and shook his head.

"Describe to me what a Level 8 means, Norm."

"Level 8 angels are wise souls that have been around for a very long time, and thus they have abilities that others at lower levels don't have. In other words, this person, a woman, that we're assigning you, is called an Intuitive."

"Oh baloney!" exclaimed Jimmy with a wave of his hand. "I don't believe in that stuff."

Norm let out a deep laugh and said, "Oh, you have so much to learn. But, hey, it's been a long day-night for you, so let me leave you with a file of this Level 8 angel for you to read and review. And I'll now take you down to your place, known as a cloud cube."

Jimmy followed Norm, and they glided along as if they were on an airport walkway. While they were moving, he noticed other people gliding by and observed that no one had wings. Some had interesting-looking backpack contraptions on their backs, but no wings. "How ironic," he murmured.

Jimmy also noticed that they seemed to be moving downward. They ended up going down a long hallway and finally came to the smallest, most boring room he had ever been in. It looked like a dorm room, but with no finesse to it. It held just a desk and a chair.

Jimmy exclaimed, "This looks like a monk's room!" Everything was white, no matter where he looked. "Where do I sleep? Where's the phone and the TV?"

"There is no TV or phone. We don't need them in Heaven, Jimmy."

"Okay, then what on Earth—or should I say Heaven—will I be *doing* all day?" Jimmy asked sarcastically.

Norm tossed him the file and said, "Reading, Jimmy. It's a wonderful thing to do—that is, when you're not snooze-dozing." He started to walk out the door.

"Excuse me, little man, but what is snooze-dozing?"

Norm slowly turned and looked seriously at Jimmy "Because of our responsibilities to those we guard, we don't sleep. We nap, otherwise known as 'resting our eyes.' Thus we can quickly be alert, since we never know when we'll be called upon and needed. Remember, Jimmy, your assignment is everything— twenty-four hours a day if needed."

"Okay, little man, whatever you say—but where do I snooze-doze?" Jimmy looked very tired at that point.

Norm felt bad that he hadn't shown him that part "Oh, Jimmy! I forgot to tell you. This is the best part of your room. Lie down on the floor.'

"On the cloud floor?"

"Yes—go ahead,"

Jimmy sighed noisily and then lay down. Within seconds he felt that he had fallen onto a bed of marshmallows. The floor was so fluffy, soft, warm, and comfy.

"Wow, Norm, this is so comfortable, I don't want to get up!"

Norm chuckled. "Well, you must, because I need you to at least glance at the file now and to let me know if you have any immediate questions."

Jimmy got up quickly with a sigh. "Okay, hand it over." He opened the file, and his immediate outburst was "Who the *hell* is Maura?"

Norm said firmly, "You must stop saying *hell*, Jimmy! It will be a setback for you to move ahead in the future."

Jimmy glared at him and rolled his eyes. "Look, little man, I don't know who this woman is, and quite frankly I don't care! I need to be looking after my kids and even my ex-wives—especially since they are all going to be at my funeral. I thought that when you died you looked after all your loved ones. That's still the deal, right?"

Norm paused as his watched Jimmy look at him intently, then said, "Well, no, Jimmy, actually it's not. It's about watching over the last person you were thinking of. Now if you had been thinking about your last wife, then, yes, you would be watching over her. If you had been a good father, concerned constantly about your kids and their well-being, then, yes, you would be watching over them. And finally, if you were closer to and cared more about your entire family, then you would be watching over all of them. But, Jimmy, you were concerned about only *you* when you died last night."

"Whoa! Wait a minute there, Norm. That's *not* true. I was thinking about my brother."

"Nooo, Jimmy. Actually, you were thinking about Bob's girlfriend, as I remember it. And *that* is who Maura is—Bob's girlfriend."

Jimmy snorted and said, "You're joking, right? I mean, come on. I don't even know this woman. I never even met her!"

"Oh, you're mistaken on that as well, my friend," Norm said with a slow, knowing smile. "You actually did see her, across a crowded street once, many years ago."

"Well, I don't remember that, and I don't believe it's even true. Thus it's not significant," Jimmy snapped back.

"Actually it was significant at the time."

"Okay," sighed Jimmy. "So what? Why her? Norm, there are

probably thousands of people right now starving, in danger, dying, in need of something. Why can't I help or watch over them?"

"Because, as I explained," Norm said quietly and patiently, "whether you like it or not, you're assigned to the last person you thought of. Take, for example, a person in a car crash. Who is the last person they are thinking of? The individual they hit. And *that* is the person they end up watching over. You could say it's retribution."

"But I don't have retribution coming to me with this lady!"

"Ah, she is a lady, and a very special one at that. When you read her file, you'll find that out. Therefore, I will leave you to snooze-doze and read."

Jimmy quickly snapped, "Okay then, I'll jump right on that, Norm. Not that there is anything else to do in this room anyway. It's so boring!"

Norm walked out into the hallway, turned, and said, "Do me a favor. Close your eyes." Jimmy stood in front of him, and did as told. "Okay, now open your eyes, and turn around, and look at your dull white wall."

Jimmy turned and gasped in disbelief. Where once had been a wall was now a small cascading waterfall, similar to the one he had seen in the garden earlier. "Wow, how did that happen?"

Norm just smiled and laughed, and said, "Hey, you're in heaven now, Jimmy! Anything can happen, even a few miracles." And with that, the little man winked, bowed, and was gone in a flash down the hall.

CHAPTER 4

Learning about the Assignment

Jimmy dove onto the floor after Norm left, engulfing himself in the marshmallow-like feeling it had. With the comfy warmth surrounding him, he instantly started to doze. Even as he drifted off, he could tell that it was a much lighter sleep than when he had been on earth. *But let's face it*, Jimmy thought, *No bed every felt like this!* And with that he "rested his eyes" for a while.

When Jimmy opened his eyes later, he had no idea how long he had been napping, since heaven didn't have clocks or light and darkness. It was like being in Alaska in the summer; it was daylight all the time. Regardless of how much time he had dozed off, short or long, he felt completely refreshed and energized.

Jimmy stared for a while at the beautiful waterfall where one of his walls had been. It made such a difference in his little sterile cloud cube, having this incredible sight as well as the sound of cascading water.

Eventually he sighed, walked over to the desk, sat in the chair, and sulked as he glanced occasionally at the closed file he was supposed to read. He wished in a way that he had never seen his sister and some of his buddies, because he wanted to hang out with them something fierce. He also longed strongly for his family and kids. Jimmy wanted to be watching over them now more than ever and to make sure everyone was doing okay. He knew that the entire family was in shocked, since he had died so suddenly.

But his sister, Pat, was overseeing the funeral and the family, and thus protecting them. And Jimmy didn't know when he was going to see her again and get an update. He stared at Maura's file again and then had an idea. If he read the whole file quickly and acted interested, maybe Norm would let him go visit with his sister and hang with her when she was checking in on the family.

Jimmy quickly opened the file of Maura's first eighteen years, and started to read through it. He found himself enraptured pretty quickly by her journey in her young life. As a matter of fact, part of it truly stunned him. Jimmy thought no one could have a worse relationship with a parent than he had with his father. And he'd felt strongly all his life that no one should. After reading Maura's file, he realized someone else had. She had survived years of abuse—physical and verbal—and emotional rejection. No matter what she did, it always seemed to be the wrong thing, and no matter how she tried to fix it, it never was the right answer or action.

During these difficult years, Maura prayed every day to God, Asking why *he* had done this to her, why she was so bad, why she was so unloved. And she begged him to give her the strength and support to leave home and never go back. At an early age, she felt strongly that her purpose on earth, God's mission, was to see how long she could survive without being loved by anyone.

It was heart-wrenching for Jimmy to read this about her— that she truly believed that. There were people in her life that loved her, but she had been so beaten down by one person that she didn't see this at all in others.

After reading the first eighteen years of Maura's life, Jimmy was really impressed with her and a bit in awe of the inner strength she found daily through prayer and resolve. Though there were some happy parts in her life along the way, and she certainly didn't need to struggle financially, the best part of her story for Jimmy was at the end. For some miraculous reason, Maura's prayers to God were answered. She was going to get to escape from her environment and go away to college—a small Catholic school in a nearby suburb.

As Jimmy finished reading this good news, on the final page in the file, Norm appeared suddenly.

"What timing, little man! I was just finishing up the last page of the first file. By the way, do you have clocks up here?"

"We don't have clocks up here, because we don't need them. As you will see in time, we watch over the people on earth, thus their time *is* our time. What did you think of Maura's first eighteen years?"

Jimmy said sheepishly, "It was definitely ironic and a bit humbling to read. I never knew anyone could go through as much as I did growing up."

"Well, what you'll learn over time, as you get to know her, is that Maura is a very strong woman who has survived a great deal. As I mentioned before, if she were to die today, she would come to Heaven to be placed as a Level 8 Angel. In other words, she's at your sister's level. Furthermore, because of this level, she has a lot of powers."

Jimmy had been listening intently. "What does that mean? What type of powers?"

Norm looked at him seriously. "As I had started telling you yesterday, she's an intuitive. She can channel spirits, has telepathy, can see things happening before others do, and can read people's thoughts and feelings by touching them. As you start studying her daily, you'll see some of this magic appear, and some amazingly cool things might happen," Norm said with a grin.

"The irony is"—Norm continued as he paced around the little cube—"Maura doesn't realize the level of power she has, or if she does, she's afraid of it. But what she does know is that her powers are a gift from God to protect her all her life, and she will only use the power she has for good."

Jimmy had no comment to this. Since he didn't believe in any of that stuff, he couldn't get a handle on what it all meant. Yet he could see that Norm was a true convert, so he thought the best action was to keep his mouth shut and let Norm keep talking.

"In addition, just to forewarn you, a lot of spirit guides, and some angels who know Maura from past lives or heaven, including your sister, like to watch Maura and see how much of her magic she uses on Earth. So beware that sometimes you'll be watching over her, and visitors will come hang out to see what she'll do."

Jimmy saw his opportunity and leaped at it. "Well, speaking of visitors, when can Pat come by and hang out? Since she knows Maura, I could probably learn a lot from her."

"No, Jimmy—not yet. Give it some time," Norm said firmly.

"Look!" Jimmy exclaimed as he leaped up off the desk chair and stared down at Norm. "I read the damn file! I gave you some feedback. I even said she seemed okay in my book. I thought that, based on this, you would cut me some slack and at least let me see what's happening at my own funeral!"

"Jimmy that is what Pat is assigned to do, and quite frankly she's pretty busy. She's watching over all your family members, and you know how big of a group that is. It's an important job, and only someone at Pat's level can handle it. Besides that, it's also an exhausting job for her. She'll visit you when and if she can." Then Norm added in a booming voice, "Okay?"

Jimmy decided he'd better not push the issue any further for now. "Okay, I guess."

"Good! I need you to now read the second file—the last twenty years of Maura's life. I think you'll find this file *most* interesting. After you finish it, I need to start getting you acclimated to watching Maura daily and being comfortable around her. Your first connection with her will be coming up soon, so you need to be ready for it."

Jimmy replied brightly, "Alrighty then. Bring on the next file! I love reading about college life."

Norm did just that, and left him to focus on reading. Jimmy leaned back in his chair and opened the second installment, which started with Maura going to college and ended in the present. It was a much larger file, since it had more years to cover and thus would take longer to read. The first section started with Maura arriving on the small college campus and happily saying good-bye to her overbearing family. The first person she met was her roommate, Katharine, a Lauren Bacall look-alike. Maura's quick assessment was that she had never seen greener eyes in her life or anyone with a more voluptuous body, which she found herself quickly becoming envious of. But what Katharine had in looks, she lacked in personality. She was the most boring and studious person Maura would meet on campus, and she thought it was just her luck that this girl was her roommate.

After only a couple of weeks on campus, Maura soon discovered that Katharine was twice as envious of Maura's body and looks. Though Maura had never focused much on it, since her family did nothing but put her down, she had always wondered about modeling. It quickly became apparent that Katharine thought she should do that—and with that came a lot of jealousy. Since Maura with a tall, fashion-model body, a few small curves but shapely legs, and Katharine was a shorter, a bit overweight, fully curved woman, the tension and jealousy started to build between them.

One beautiful Sunday, while Katharine wanted complete silence in the room so she could study, and Maura was in no mood to do that, the tension became unbearable. So she left the dorm room quickly to get some fresh air and to walk off the anxiety she was feeling.

It was a gorgeous warm autumn day in what is often called Indian Summer in New England. Maura decided to walk around the whole campus and take in the beautiful scenery around the college. As she was doing this, she came across a dormitory building that she had never seen before, called Angel Hall. She was curious about what was behind the building and decided to walk around it. As she came around the other side, the vision she encountered would change her life forever.

Coming out of a side door was the most handsome man that she had ever seen. The fact that he was in a campus security uniform didn't take away from the scene either. He made Maura stop in her tracks. He was an older, tall man, but well-built with dark-brown hair and kind brown eyes.

He smiled slowly and said, "Hello."

Maura stood there transfixed and softly said hello, realizing at that moment she wasn't capable of more than one-word answers.

He spoke again, and said, "Beautiful day, isn't it?"

Maura softly answered, "Yes," and thought she must look like a dunce with the one-word answers.

He continued calmly, as if they had met several times before, and said, "May I ask where you're going?"

She answered more confidently, smiling, "Just going for a walk around campus."

He then gave her a slow once-over look from head to toe, which made her blush, but in a good way. Other men had done that to her over the years, and it always made her feel very uncomfortable. But this was different. She didn't even know his name, but she was overwhelmed with a feeling of complete trust—as if she already knew him.

Then there was a silence while they both stared at each other.

Finally Maura slowly turned to walk away. As she did this, she could *not* stop smiling. She had a grin ear to ear, and she realized that she had never felt so happy in her life. *How is this possible?* Maura turned to look back, just to see if he was a mirage. To her glee, he was still rooted to the spot, staring at her as she walked away.

This was the first encounter of Maura and Bob, and the start of a very intense emotional relationship that lasted for four solid years and beyond.

Jimmy had to put the file down. He was completely *stunned*. He never knew that Bob met Maura while he was working at one of the college campuses. In all the years from then to now, Bob had never mentioned any of this to him. To think that they had carried on an incredible romance at a Catholic college, and Jimmy had never had any clue. None of the family had— including Bob's fiancée and future wife at the time.

Jimmy picked up the file eagerly, wondering how their relationship would survive, considering the commitment Bob had already made, which he took very seriously. Still it was evident to Jimmy, and other people who knew Bob, how miserable he was over the years. Jimmy quickly realized that he was reading a romance novel spanning the next several years of Maura's life.

When she finally realized that there was no way Bob was going to give in to their love for one another and change things in his life to be with her, Maura moved on. But moving on wasn't easy, and over the years she met a string of loser men who did not accomplishing anything other than capturing her heart and breaking it to pieces. And during those years of hurt, she lost more and more confidence in herself and eventually let her model figure fall apart. She became a plain-looking overweight woman. Maura just didn't care anymore, and she resigned herself to the fact that she might be alone for the rest of her life.

Then one night, while depressed, Maura decided to pick up the phone and call Bob. She had not talked to him in ten years, yet when they reconnected, it was like it had only been ten days. And the best part of all was that Bob was single and so was Maura.

Jimmy continued to read in earnest about how Maura had changed residences, men, and careers over the years but had come out a successful business woman and had overcome all the obstacles thrown at her.

When he finished reading the second installment, he had a much better understanding of the relationship between his brother and Maura. How deep the connection was, how much they had survived separately and together, and most importantly, how much they still loved one another.

Jimmy found himself more than envious as he read about their reunion, because he realized what they had together was more special than most people encountered in an entire lifetime. He certainly hadn't found his soulmate; that had eluded him more than a few times. He had looked all his life for someone like Maura. *And to think my brother had this woman right under my nose all these years!*

But one thing that Jimmy could see from reading Maura's file was that from the start, she understood her relationship with Bob was a special gift. Even at eighteen, she had the insight to know that in her lifetime she would never meet or love anyone more completely than Bob.

Just then Norm appeared out of nowhere at the entrance to Jimmy's cloud cube. "So, Jimmy, have you finished the second installment?"

"Yes." Jimmy nodded quickly.

"So, what do you think now?"

"I've never known for all those years that my brother had a relationship with Maura and that she loved him so much."

Norm smiled gently and said, "Well, it's a testament to the strength of their love that they just picked up where they left off years ago, as if nothing had changed or happened. Unfortunately your death has deeply affected your brother, and he has decided to tell Maura he wants to put their relationship on hold for a while." "No! He can't do that to Maura! Does she even know I've died?"

"No, not yet. They were supposed to go out the night you died, and Maura thinks that he stood her up, especially when she called him recently, and he said he needed his space."

Jimmy sighed, exasperated. "What Bob needs now is Maura!"

Norm nodded in quick agreement "Unfortunately Bob doesn't have the time to see her, even if he wanted to right now. The family is pulling him in fifty directions."

"So, Norm, when am I actually going to see Maura myself?" Jimmy asked eagerly.

"Actually, right now. Follow me," Norm said, smiling.

They glided down a few hallways and finally came to a comfy area that looked like a large den, and it was much nicer than the cloud cube Jimmy had been cooped up in.

Norm stated, "This is where you will be spending a lot of your time now, studying Maura, and getting used to her daily routine. Now close your eyes again, and focus on an image of Maura, based on the description you read in her file." Norm waited a couple of minutes and said, "Okay, Jimmy, open your eyes and look at the wall across the room."

When he opened his eyes and looked at the space where there had been a white wall, he couldn't believe what he was now seeing: Maura, live on earth, sitting on her bed, reading a book.

Norm was watching his reaction and quickly explained, "This place is calling a viewing room. There are several all over heaven; they are used by angels constantly to view those they guard. This is the closest one to your cloud cube. Now, Jimmy, I have to say I am highly impressed that you were able to create such a strong image of Maura on your first try. And you're able to see her live now, though I have to admit I helped out a bit." Norm added with a wink.

"Now your assignment is to watch over Maura, and as boring as this may get at times, you'll be studying her through this viewing screen for now. Soon, when I feel you're ready, I'll send you down to be with her. Okay?"

"Sure!" Jimmy responded, happy to be moving along with his assignment and to hang in a much nicer room.

Thus, from that day onward, Jimmy hung out in the viewing room to study Maura. What surprised him was how many spirit guides and angel would drop in to watch Maura with him. When he asked why, they just smiled and said nothing or replied, "Because she's a special earth angel."

Jimmy found this earth angel worshiping" annoying because

A. so far Maura's life, in his eyes, was very boring and in no need of watching over;

B. he'd rather be watching with another powerful angel, like his sister, Pat, who he missed; and

C. these angel visitors never came to check in or hang out with him or give him any tips on Heaven.

Jimmy was also finding out something that really surprised him: being in Heaven could get really lonely. He thought maybe it was because he was a Level 1 spirit guide or because he needed to adjust overall, but it felt like solitary confinement. And the more he thought about it, the more he decided to complain to Norm the next time he saw him. If he was going to spend day after day just watching Maura live an ordinary, sometimes boring life, that wasn't going to work. He was determined to push to be assigned to someone else.Norm periodically checked in briefly on him during the first couple of weeks to see how things were progressing. And finally, on one of those visits, Jimmy decided to lay it all out on the line. He told Norm how bored and frustrated he was, how he felt like he was accomplishing nothing watching over Maura. "Why waste my time on her when I could be helping my family or other people who really need help?"

Norm listened to his tirade patiently and finally replied, "Look, Jimmy, I know it's a bit of an adjustment to be in heaven now, and yes, at the moment Maura is not leading a very exciting life, but things will get more interesting shortly."

Jimmy let out a loud sigh and said firmly, "I don't know how much more I can take of this. I don't think I'm cut out for this spirit guide stuff!"

"Well, this *IS* what we do up here—some more than others," Norm quickly retorted and then left the viewing room.

Jimmy watched him leave and realized he had no idea what Norm really did. He had never asked him. All he knew was that Norm seemed very important, everyone seemed to know him, and he was always very busy as well. Jimmy made a mental note that he needed to ask more questions when he saw Norm again.

As he was reflecting on this, a warm light engulfed the viewing room. Jimmy felt the warmth surround him, and he had to close his eyes because of the glare. When he opened them, his sister was standing right in front of him.

Smiling, she said, "Hello, Jimmy!"

"Pat! It's so good to see you," Jimmy exclaimed.

"I know. I'm sorry I haven't been able to visit you sooner."

"Well," Jimmy replied with a sulking look on his face, "I haven't been doing anything, so I have all the time in the world to chat and visit with you."

"Oh, Jimmy, don't say that! It's truly so amazing to be here compared to earth. It just takes time to adjust. Soon you'll be fine."

"So, where have you been? What have you been doing?" Jimmy quickly asked.

"I've been watching over our big family since you've died. Been really busy with that." Pat sighed.

"How's everyone doing? How was the funeral?" Jimmy said, looking concerned.

"Badly unfortunately—especially Mom, Bobby, and your kids. Quite honestly, I was so busy watching over them at the funeral that I paid no attention to your most recent ex-wife."

"Good," Jimmy retorted. "She's a total piece of work—and a waste of time and energy anyways."

"Well, had I been paying attention, I could have tried to prevent her scoffing over a thousand dollars you had in your wallet when you died," Pat said annoyed. "Can you believe that on the day of the funeral she *took it*?"

"No way! You're kidding me. That total lowlife." Jimmy started pacing around the viewing room. "Had I been there, like I wanted to be, I would have made sure that never happened. Damn it!"

"Jimmy, calm down!" Pat stated firmly. "You weren't allowed to be there, per Norm, so get over it."

"Okay, okay" Jimmy stopped pacing and turned to Pat. "So, seriously, how is everyone else doing?"

"Everyone is still in shock overall, but that's not why I'm here visiting you."

"Really? Okay, why then?"

"I'm here to take you on your first angel journey," Pat said excitedly and clapped her hands quickly together.

"Wow, coolio! Where are we going?"

"Well, Jimmy, where is Maura going tonight?" Pat quickly asked.

"Nowhere, Pat. Trust me on that," Jimmy replied in a flat tone.

"Okay then, let's change that right now," Pat stated with a twinkle in her eye as she turned toward the viewing screen.

At that exact moment, Maura's phone rang. It was Bob on the other end, whom she hadn't heard from in weeks. By the end of the conversation, they had agreed to get together that night and go out somewhere fun.

When the conversation was done, which Jimmy had been listening to intently, he jumped up and down. "Hot damn!

Now we're talking!" Then he quickly turned to his sister in amazement. "Did you make that all happen?"

Pat laughed and said, "Oh, Jimmy, it's just angel magic. So are you ready for your first angel adventure with me?"

Jimmy quickly replied with a grin, "I'd go anywhere with you, kid!"

CHAPTER 5

The First Connection

Over the next hour, Pat showed Jimmy how to slide down to Earth and get back to Heaven. Though they didn't have much time to go through the rules of engagement, and how to get back to Heaven quickly if he needed to, Pat did the best she could to give him a crash course. She wished she could teach him to fly, but since he was a Level 1 Spirit Guide, he didn't have wings. And Pat wasn't sure she wanted him to know that she did, so she kept them hidden as best she could from him—in the knapsack on her back.

Jimmy was beyond excited to be learning how to leave Heaven. Essentially, the plan was to go down a long, narrow tunnel to earth. Or, as Pat said, "Think of it as a huge slide." Once there, they would find Bob and Maura and hang out with them for the night. The coolest part for Jimmy was that once they were on Earth, they were invisible. So he could be hanging out next to Bob, and Bob would never even know he was there.

Finally Pat felt Jimmy was ready and—if nothing else—very eager to get going. So she let Jimmy go down the tunnel slide first, and she hung on from behind. When they landed, it was right outside Bob's house—just as he was coming out of it and getting into his car.

Pat whispered, "Hurry, Jimmy! Slip into the back seat of the car before he shuts the door!" Jimmy moved quickly and slid into the back with Pat right behind him, just as Bob shut the door and started the engine.

Jimmy was so ecstatic he was almost speechless. He could not believe he was back on earth, and most importantly, seeing his brother again. He turned to Pat and whispered, "Can Bobby hear, see, or sense us?"

Pat shook her head. "As I told you upstairs, no—he can't. You have no idea how frustrating it's been for me. So many times I have been right at Bob's side when he needed me most or missed me terribly, and he never knew or sensed it."

Jimmy looked at his brother and then back to Pat with a stunned expression and stated, "I never ever thought I'd see my brother again. Thank you so much for making this happen!"

Pat smiled. "I'm glad I could make you happy. I've watch over Bob every day since I died. Thus when you're with me, you can see Bob, and that's why we're here. Actually that's one of the reasons. The other reason is Maura."

Pat continued, "Now Maura, on the other hand, senses everything! You have no idea how lucky you are to be assigned to her. And hopefully you'll see why tonight."

Jimmy snorted and said, "Huh, we'll see about that. So far I'm not impressed."

"That's because you haven't seen her magic, Jimmy. She and I were like twins in Heaven. We had the same level of magic up there, and when you combine our magic together, there's no stopping us," Pat said with a laugh.

"So you know Maura?" Jimmy asked incredulously,

"Not on Earth this time. But we've been in Heaven at the same time in the past, between lives. We had a lot of good times together, since we were at the same level. And we were both brought down to earth this time as earth angels and as a test to see how long we could last on earth without being unconditionally loved by one person. Sadly Maura has really struggled with that over the years."

By this point Bob had driven to the meeting place to wait for Maura. When Maura arrived a few minutes later, she was glowing with happiness. She leaped out of her car and ran into Bob's arms to give him a big hug and kiss. But immediately upon seeing Bob close up, Maura sensed something was different. There was a strained look on his face, and he seemed slow to smile, to react to her affectionate greeting, and to see her overall. He did tell Maura that she looked great, which made her happy, but her instincts told her something was off.

As they drove away, Bob seemed quiet and very subdued, so Maura decided she would chat up a storm with him, to see if that would lighten his mood and get him to laugh.

Jimmy turned to his sister at this point and burst out, "Why hasn't Bob told her about me?"

"You know your brother," Pat sighed. "The great communicator! It's always been his downfall."

"But it's Maura we're talking about here."

Pat shook her head sadly and said, "It doesn't matter. It will take him most of the night to tell her. That's why you have to help Maura. She's going to need it."

As Jimmy turned to watch Maura more closely, he could sense that she was starting to panic. She realized something was very wrong at that point, and naturally she thought it had to do with her. She assumed that Bob's distant and distracted actions during the night meant that he wanted to break up with her. He was definitely acting odd—pulling off the side of the road and having her walk with him to an abandon railroad track stop that had no lights.

Even Jimmy thought this was a bit weird, and he started to worry for her.

But all Bob wanted to do once he got her there was to hold her for a long time and not say anything. It was then, as this happened, that Maura could feel waves of immense sadness going through him. And she thought, *Oh no, he wants to break up with me and doesn't know how to tell me!*

When they got back into the car, she was fighting back tears, trying not to cry in front of him.

Jimmy looked at Pat and said, "Whoa! She's spiraling into a big-time depression out of nowhere. And she thinks Bob doesn't love her anymore, but that's not the case! What can I do to help her?'"

"You're on, Jimmy!" Pat said. "Here's your first assignment: connect with Maura—right now."

"But how?" Jimmy responded, confused.

His sister smiled and said, "Never forget this: through music."

"Through music?" Jimmy asked

"Yes! It's how all of us in Heaven, including God, communicate with Maura. It works. And the key is, she knows this." Pat stated quite factually.

Jimmy looked at her stupefied. "Come on."

"I told you how special Maura is, and now you're going to see a glimpse, first hand, of what I'm talking about," Pat said with a grand gesture of her hand toward Maura.

"You're gonna help me, right?" Jimmy quickly asked.

"Nope. It's all you, buddy. All you need to do is channel into a radio station in Bob's car, and turn one of the stations into a jukebox of your musical choices. But remember this: pick songs that will have meaning to Bob and some that Maura will like as well."

Having said this, she turned and focused on Maura in the car, and Jimmy watched in amazement as Maura said, as if on cue, "Gee, Bob, let's find some good tunes to listen to." Then he stared in disbelief as his sister guided Maura's hand to a station and stopped.

Pat turned to Jimmy, smiling. "Here's a totally clear, open channel. So go ahead, bro. Knock yourself out and fill it up with some good tunes! Anything you can think of will instantly go in there and start playing."

Instantly Jimmy thought of a song from the sixties, and it came on the radio—right then and there. From then on, he couldn't stop thinking of different songs, ones that he and his brother grew up listening to and ones Maura knew of as well. Before long, Bob was singing along to the songs, telling Maura they were his favorites, and he hadn't heard them in years. She smiled and started singing too.

At that point, Pat turned to Jimmy and said, "Have a good time tonight. You're doing great! I need to leave now, but trust me, if you need anything, Norm will be at your side in a second—including when you're ready to go back to heaven. Okay?"

"Okay, sis. Thanks for everything." Jimmy turned back to the radio station, thinking he didn't care if he ever went back to heaven.

Pat was relieved to see that Jimmy wasn't upset that she was going. And because he was distracted, he didn't turn in time to see her open her huge, beautiful rainbow wings and fly away.

Jimmy was too focused on having a blast with the radio station to think twice about where his sister went. He had gotten Bob to forget all his troubles, get into the music, and drive all the way down Route 6 on Cape Cod with his favorite girl. And Maura was happy because she could sense Bob's mood lightening. She cuddled up to him as his drove, knowing not to ask where they were going exactly, because Bob always made it a surprise.

They drove a long way on Route 6, and Bob finally pulled into a secluded beach area in a town named Dennis. They got out of the car, pulled a big blanket out of the trunk, and walked out onto the soft sand. Maura spread the blanket out on the beach, and she and Bob lay down and stared up at the big, bright moon and stars.

Bob pulled Maura close to him, gave her a long kiss, and then just held her close for a long time without saying anything. Maura sensed again the overwhelming sadness emanating from him as they lay together. But because she thought it had to do with her, she couldn't ask the simple question "What's wrong?"

What she did know was not to push him, and she decided not to turn the time on the beach into a romp in the sand. Gut instinct told Maura to just let it alone and let Bob lead where he wanted things to go. And it became obvious quickly that he just wanted to hold her, to take in the beauty of the surrounding ocean, and to chill.

Meantime, in the back of Maura's head, she could hear a male voice insisting, "Ask him; ask him what's wrong!" But she pushed it out of her head. Jimmy was actually chanting this to her, but he had no way of knowing whether he was connecting with her or not—and he was getting exhausted from trying.

Bob and Maura stayed on the beach for a long time, just talking, cuddling, and reminiscing about the past. Finally they decided to head back home, since it was starting to get cold and very late.

When Bob started the car, the radio came back on and was finishing up a tune. Just as Jimmy was thinking, *What's the point of all this?* the first connection happened. As a new song started, Maura turned and said, "Bob, we need to remember this radio station. It's great!"

He replied, "I know. Funny, but I never remember hearing it before."

"Well, what are the call letters?"

"I don't know. We'll have to pay better attention."

That's when it clicked for Maura. She turned to Bob with a stunned look on her face and said, "They haven't said the call letters all night! It's FCC regulations to announce them so many times an hour, and they have never said them once."

Maura turned to look out the window and was silent while she thought that through. She realized that in the two hours they had been in the car, driving down to the Cape, there had not been one commercial either. That's when Maura smiled and realized that something very special had happened. She decided not to bring it to Bob's attention though—she didn't want to freak him out. She wasn't sure he would understand the special music connection she had with heaven.

Jimmy started jumping up and down in the back seat of the car, shouting, "She got it. She got it! Hot damn."

At that moment Bob turned to Maura and said, "There's something I need to tell you, hon."

Maura's heart stopped. She turned, seriously looked in his eyes, expecting the worst, and said, "What is it?" And that's when he told her that his brother had died suddenly two weeks before, the night they were to go out.

Maura breathed a sigh of relief and instantly understood everything: his sadness, unfocused attention and actions, distant behavior as well as his melancholy mood. Though she was hurt that Bob hadn't told her earlier, she understood how hard it was for him to share his feelings, and her heart went out to him. She let him talk about how it happened, how bothered he was with the suddenness of Jimmy's heart attack, how he had planned to see Jimmy that next day, and about the funeral and all that transpired there.

At some point, Maura realized that the music had stopped completely because they could no longer get a clear signal on the radio channel—or so she thought. No matter how hard she tried, she couldn't get the station to come back. Just then it hit her what was so special about all this: she knew it somehow related to Jimmy. She didn't say a word to Bob about her thoughts—she knew he would never believe her.

By that point, Bob and Maura were getting back home very late, at two. As Jimmy was wondering what to do next, Norm mysteriously appeared next to the car and said to him, "You did great on your first angel assignment. I am very pleased!"

Jimmy grinned ear to ear. "Thanks, little man! It was *so* cool. I got to hang with my sister, see my brother, and connect through to Maura."

Norm quickly said, "Ah, don't jump to conclusions just yet about connecting. Maura hasn't completely processed the event and figured it out yet."

"Oh, Norm, I think she will," Jimmy stated confidently, like he had become an instant true believer in her capabilities.

Norm smiled in return and said, "Okay then. We have to get going now and zoom back to heaven."

Jimmy looked at him bewildered and said, "How are we going to do that, Norm? We can't go back up a slide!"

Norm nodded. "Follow me to that street light in the parking lot." Jimmy did, and Norm told him to stand under the light and grab ahold of his arm. Norm looked at him, winked, and said, "This is how easy it is to get back up to Heaven." He looked into the light and said, "Up!" and off they went together at a fast speed. All Jimmy remembered was starting to be lifted up; the next thing he knew, he was standing back in the viewing room.

Meanwhile, after saying goodnight to Bob, Maura got in her car and started to drive home, which would take her another half hour. She drove along the highway in a happy but pensive mood. Before she got into her car, Bob had told her he didn't know when they would get together again and that he needed his space to process and mourn the death of his brother.

Maura understood this, but at the same time, as always, she felt that she never saw enough of him. Thus she realized it could be weeks, if not months, before they connected again. It was already August, with September fast approaching, as well as Bob's fiftieth birthday.

As she drove, Maura's mind drifted over the events of the evening in detail and settled on the radio and song list. In her gut, she knew that someone in heaven was trying to send her a message. That's the way it had worked for years, when angels—and sometimes even God—wanted to get her attention. She knew the signs as well as the special songs.

No, she thought suddenly, *that's not completely right. Someone in Heaven is trying to reach Bob through me! But why?* None of her special songs had been played. All the songs were from Bob's era, not hers, though occasionally some from hers would be mixed in. The oddest part was that the songs were all rare ones that hadn't been heard on mainstream radio in years. And more importantly, she knew there were no commercials and no FCC call letter announcements. So someone in heaven definitely was trying to get through. But who?

Maura arrived at her suburban home in the woods, and as she pulled into the driveway, she wondered about the voice she had distinctly heard in her head when she was on the beach. It had said, "Ask him. Ask him!" It was definitely a male voice, but not one she recognized. Then again, Maura said to herself, scoffing, "How do you recognize voices from the spirit world?" It bugged her enough to be troubled into thinking that maybe she was just starting to hear voices in her head all of a sudden.

Maura let out a loud sigh as she walked into the house. As she tiredly trudged upstairs to the master bedroom, she said out loud, "For all I know, that was Jimmy's voice." She quickly pushed that out of her mind, saying to herself, "Come on! You don't even know the guy." With this finally thought, she quickly whipped off her clothes, shut off the lights, and dove into her sleigh bed. Before she could process another thought, she was fast asleep.

Jimmy was sitting in the viewing room, and when he heard Maura say his name, he leaped up and started high-fiving Norm. "She said it, Norm! She knows! Maura really knows."

Norm laughed and said, "We've been telling you that Maura has a unique gift. She's a special Earth Angel, Jimmy."

Jimmy couldn't stand still, he was so excited. He started pacing around the room. "Man, this is just *great*. I can't believe she figured out the connection so fast! What do I do next? What's my next assignment?"

Norm replied, "Let her get some rest, and you as well. There will be plenty of time and things you can do once you really connect with her and she knows you're her spirit guide."

Jimmy looked at Norm, perplexed, and said, "How do I make her know that I exist?"

Norm said, "You need her to get a visual of you in her mind, through what we call a daydream, which happens not when she's sleeping, but as she's waking up. So, for now, go snooze-doze for a bit. You've had a very exciting night. We'll connect again when Maura starts to wake up, which—trust me—will not be for another twelve hours. This woman loves her beauty sleep!" He laughed.

Jimmy laughed as well and said, "You're telling me! And why do you think I'm so bored all the time? It can be like watching paint dry just being assigned to her. You really need to find me something else to do, Norm."

"Jimmy, focus on tonight. You should be really happy with what you've accomplished. I'll see you tomorrow. Have a good snooze-doze," Norm reiterated as he turned to leave the viewing room.

Jimmy gently smiled and said, "Thanks for everything, little man! Good-night."

CHAPTER 6

The Second Connection—The Dream

L ater the next morning, Norm went to visit Jimmy in his cloud cube, only to find it empty. So he glided down the hallways until he came to the viewing room, and there he found Jimmy, snooze-dozing on the floor.

Norm quietly said, "Jimmy!"

Jimmy immediately flashed open his eyes and sat up quickly. "Is it time yet? Is Maura awake?" He glanced at the viewing screen, only to see that Maura was still fast asleep.

Norm said confidently, "She'll be awake soon. You decided not to snooze-doze in your room?"

Jimmy smiled sheepishly. "I didn't want to miss out on my next opportunity."

Norm replied, "Well, that will be happening shortly." As he said it, he looked at the screen and could see Maura starting to stir a bit. "Okay, here is your next assignment, if you're ready. And it's a tricky one."

Jimmy quickly said, "I'm ready."

"Maura is coming out of a deep REM sleep now and is floating in and out of a lighter sleep and consciousness," Norm said. "This means she can dream, be aware of her dream, and remember it as well. You need to catch her during this light sleep phase and insert a dream situation that she'll remember when she wakes up. Thus she'll know that she saw you in the dream."

Jimmy asked, "Any situation?"

Norm replied, "Yes. But if I were you, I would try to make it something that has to do with Bob, since you want to connect with him as well."

"Why do I have to do that?"

"Remember that Maura might *not* believe this dream. Therefore you have to make it a situation that Bob will remember, so that when she tells him about this, he will completely understand."

Jimmy was quiet for a minute as he thought about what Norm had just told him. "How much time do I have?"

"Very little—actually under five minutes. But I know you can do this, Jimmy," Norm said encouragingly. "Just focus!"

Jimmy closed his eyes and thought about various events that had happened in his life, but he kept discarding them because they didn't connect well with Maura's life in any way.

Norm jumped in and said, "Come on, Jimmy, you have very little time left! She's starting to wake up."

Just then Jimmy thought of a perfect scenario. "Okay, Norm, I'm ready!"

"Great! Now focus totally on Maura and start to play out the dream in your head like it's a movie."

At that moment, Maura started to stir in bed and could feel herself waking up, but she turned over and murmured to herself, "Nooo, it's too early!" and started to drop back off into a light sleep and dream.

Maura dreamed she was in Boston with Bob at a small rustic bar. It was one of those places that has low ceilings and a very old, authentic wood-beam structure. The bar was lively and crowded with people everywhere, hanging close together. At the far end of the bar was a tiny dance floor, and a live band was playing cover songs that night.

Bob was coming back from the bar with a Sam Adam beer for each of them, and as Maura watched him walking toward her, she suddenly heard a man nearby say, "Hi there!" As she turned her head a bit to the left to see where the sound had come from, suddenly she saw a handsome, Dean Martin lookalike man, in a leather jacket, leaning against the wooden post and beam pole closest to Maura, smiling at her.

Before she could open her mouth to say hello, this man hurriedly said, "No! Don't say anything out loud! I can hear you perfectly in my head as you think of things to say." Maura stared at him in stunned silence. She couldn't have said anything if she wanted to, because as he spoke, she realized that *this* was the voice she had heard repeatedly saying, "Ask him!" the night before.

The man gently said, "Don't *be* afraid, and don't *look* afraid. Bob will immediately pick up on that. He's coming toward you now. Look at him and smile, like nothing out of the ordinary is happening."

Maura did as she was told and couldn't believe what Bob did next. He stopped in front of her and leaned on the same post and beam that Jimmy was at, but on the other side. Maura could now clearly see them both, the dapper-looking Dean Martin type confidently looking like he owned the whole bar, and Bob, the more distinguished, handsome, and taller man. But if she looked at them quickly, she could see the resemblance in their profiles. And that's when it struck Maura like a thunderbolt what was happening. Her eyes went wide and she thought, *You're Jimmy!*

Jimmy nodded toward her with a brim-of-the-hat gesture and a grin, saying, "Yes, ma'am, that would be me!"

At that moment, Bob looking concerned. "Maura, what's wrong? You look very pale." To Maura's relief, he had not seen or heard Jimmy.

Maura smoothly said, "Oh, Bob, you missed it! Some old guy behind you just grab at some young babe's butt that he didn't know, as he was walking up to the bar, and she slapped him."

Bob laughed and turned around to see what she meant.

Jimmy chuckled and said, "Quick and good answer, Maura!"

Maura sighed and thought, *Why are you here? Why are you doing this? Bob can't see you, right?*

"No, he can't. You're the only one in this whole bar that can," Jimmy proudly stated.

That's just great! Maura thought.

At that point, Bob turned back around. Jimmy could see Maura getting that wide-eyed, panicked look on her face again, so he quickly said, "Dance with me!"

Maura shouted in her head, *What? Are you CRAZY? I can't dance with you. I'll look like a nut job, because no one else can see you!*

"Ahhh, but Maura, you've never danced with me!" stated Jimmy with a confident air. "I'll make it look like you're dancing for Bob. You know how much he'll love that. Come on! Listen to the music." And with that, Jimmy quickly spun her around.

Maura could feel herself being spun, even though she couldn't feel Jimmy's arms. Just then the band's lead singer started singing, "I'm not missing you at all, since you've been gone," a rendition of the John Waite song. Before she could object or understand what was happening, she was dancing and being led gracefully in turns, twists, and cool dance steps by Jimmy.

Meanwhile, Bob couldn't take his eyes off of her. He always loved to watch Maura dance, and when they first met, he use to have her dance for him whenever there was an opportunity. He always felt that she should have been a professional dancer.

And Maura felt like she was dancing with Fred Astaire. No one had ever taken such command and control of her every move, and Jimmy knew how to guide her from one step to the next as smooth as silk. She was doing dance steps she never knew she was capable of. She couldn't help but start laughing, she was having so much fun.

Jimmy laughed with her as well. There was nothing better than dancing. It's what he absolutely loved to do. In addition, it was the first fun he'd had since being in Heaven, and who would have guessed it would be with Bob's girl? Her incredible blue eyes and smile mesmerized him. He didn't want the song to end, or the dance.

The music stopped, and Maura smiled at Bob, who told her, "You're still the most amazing dancer I know, Maura!" Then she glanced at Jimmy and thought, "Why? Why now? And why *me*?!"

Jimmy replied, "Because you are the only one I can connect to Bob through. I'm your guardian angel now, Maura—full-time. I want you to tell Bob this, and let him know what just happened. And tell him that, unlike the song, I *am* missing him."

Alarmed, Maura thought, *I can't do that! How would I explain all this?*

Jimmy replied, "You'll find a way, kiddo. But look, I'm eyeing some beautiful babes across the room on the dance floor, and I think I need to go check them out. Man, being dead has its benefits!" Jimmy laughed. "By the way, make sure you and Bob don't leave here too soon, because I want to get a chance to dance with these hot ladies for a while." With that, Jimmy glided easily through the crowd to the dance floor.

Maura was too upset to reply or stop him. She looked back at Bob and started to get choked up. *Tell Bob that I just saw, talked to, and danced with his dead brother? Inconceivable! He would never believe me, and it would just upset him.* With that thought, Maura started to feel overwhelmed with emotion.

She quickly said, "Bob, I need to get some air. It's really hot in here. I'll be back." Before Bob could say anything, Maura pushed her way through the crowd quickly and went out the front door. She frantically turned left then right, looking for the alleyway, and once she found it, she ran down toward the end. Once there, she leaned against the cool wall, taking deep breaths and trying her best not to cry.

Maura couldn't believe what had just happened. *It isn't fair, damn it! Why me? Why am I the only freak in the whole bar that could not only see a spirit but also dance with him and then have a telepathic conversation with him as well! And what if this wasn't Jimmy? What if I am becoming delusional and completely losing my mind?* With that thought, she started to breathe quicker and deeper.

At that moment, Maura bolted awake in her bed. She found herself breathing quickly and covered in sweat. She couldn't believe the dream she'd just had and knew that, though it was disturbing at best, she must remember it. So she sat cross-legged in her bed, thinking through and replaying as many of the details of the dream as she could remember.

Everything in her mind said, "It was just a stupid dream; calm down," but in her gut she knew that wasn't the case. She knew intuitively that she had just met Jimmy—that is, if the dream was to be believed. Maura sighed and thought, *This has never happened to me before. I have never been able to connect with a spirit guide, except once on an Ouija board, but that doesn't count. All the times I tried and couldn't connect with my grandmother, when I needed her—yet this happens instead.*

She stayed in bed another half hour, thinking about all of it. And in the end, she came to the conclusion that she had another psychic talent that she never knew she had: channeling spirits from the other side.

At that point, Jimmy turned to Norm and said, "Wow! That was really intense. I felt like I was back in the bar I had visited with Bob a couple of years ago, like it was yesterday. The difference was that this time I could really dance and not feel out of breath or tired. I actually felt young again. It was awesome!"

Norm smiled and said, "So then being dead isn't that bad, is it? As you said to Maura, it has its benefits."

Jimmy replied, "Ya know, little man, it's okay. I'm getting used to it. And I'm realizing you're right about Maura. She definitely is something special. So, what's next?"

Norm chuckled. "Glad to see you're so eager, Jimmy! But for now, let Maura digest all that's happened. We need to give it a couple of weeks before we try to reconnect with her." Jimmy was disappointed with this answer, but he quietly said, "Okay" and left it at that.

Norm looked at him seriously and said, "Realize this, Jimmy: You were *very* successful in a very short period of time to connect with Maura. She knows where you are and who you are—her guardian angel. And that makes your second assignment a great success!" With that, Norm turned and was gone.

Jimmy watched him leave, and was pleased with how well things had gone, and more importantly how happy Norm seemed with him. *Keep this up,* he thought, *and maybe I'll be free to visit with others sooner than later.* He smiled contently.

Over the next week, Maura tried to take in what had happened. She realized and accepted that for whatever reason, Jimmy, Bob's brother, was her guardian angel and was trying to connect to Bob through her. Maybe that wasn't such a bad thing after all, but she needed to find a way to tell Bob.

Maura still wanted to know why though. She knew there must be a special reason this happened, considering the fact that she had never connected with a spirit guide before. She was determined to get an answer to that one. What Maura didn't know was that Jimmy was assigned to her for an infinite amount of time, no matter how boring it might get.

And boring it was for Jimmy. Maura led an ordinary life of work, eat, sleep, socializing with friends, and some travel. BUT exciting it was not. She didn't go out partying a lot, and she never went to dance clubs—Jimmy's favorite hangout spot. In his mind, things could be a lot more interesting if Maura looked around her and noticed the twenty-eight-year-old guy at work who had the hots for her and who wanted to put the moves on her. But Maura was oblivious to anyone but Bob.

Thus, one day, when Jimmy thought he would lose his mind from boredom, he summoned Norm to his cloud cube. When Norm showed up, Jimmy was pacing and looking agitated. Norm apprehensively said, "Jimmy, what's going on?"

"Look, Norm, I cannot take this anymore! You need to assign me to someone else or someone additional to Maura. I could be helping so many other people, but *no,* I'm stuck with this woman who leads the most unexciting, ordinary life I've ever seen. And the fact that my brother doesn't seem to have any desire to see Maura more frequently is driving me crazy. Doesn't he have any idea how much he is hurting her? Why can't he figure out or see just how much she loves him? Maura deserves better than this, and I'm really upset Bob is acting like he doesn't know who she is deep down inside."

"Jimmy, calm down!" Norm replied. "I told you it would get boring at times. As for your brother, WHY do you think you've been assigned to her? It is to be her protector against all the hurt he will inflict on her over time—that's why. You cannot see into the future like I can, but trust me, she is really going to need you down the road as things get tougher for her. There will be events that unfold that she will have no control over, and yet she will get hurt in the end by Bob, because he will not communicate with her when he should. You will play a very important role in helping her get through all that will come to pass. You have to trust me on this."

Jimmy quieted down upon hearing what Norm had to say. He believed him and wanted to ask more about what would happen, but something told him not to go there. Instead he said to Norm, "Okay, I believe you, *but* that doesn't solve my immediate problem: boredom. Norm, something has to give."

Norm smiled slowly and said, "I've been expecting this from you, Jimmy. You're someone who loves being active, and more importantly, being around other people, especially fun people. Therefore I do have a solution for you."

Jimmy said eagerly, "What? I'm ready for anything!"

Norm chuckled. "Have you ever played poker?"

"Yeah, I have—years ago though. I'm pretty rusty. Why?"

"Because I'm going to let you in on a little secret up here in Heaven. But you have to promise me that you don't let any earthlings you encounter know about it, because I'm not sure it would go over very well down there."

"Okay, little man, my lips are sealed!" Jimmy stated firmly.

"Well, the secret is that many angels, like you, get

bored—especially those just assigned to one person. Being a guardian angel isn't always what it's cracked up to be. So it was finally realized that we had to come up with a solution that would pass the time slowly and hold people's interest. And that solution was *poker*!"

Jimmy laughed. "No way! You're allowed to play poker in Heaven?"

Norm nodded. "Yes sir, you are—as long as it's approved by someone like myself. So I approve you to play poker—in the viewing room, of course—as long as you still keep an eye on Maura."

Jimmy grinned and exclaimed, "Hot damn! That's just fine with me!"

Norm replied, "Okay then. Let's go back to the viewing room and set things up." With that, they both glided down the hallway quickly.

When Jimmy walked into the viewing room, he couldn't believe his eyes. In front of him, seated around an authentic poker table, were all his buddies from the Vietnam War—the ones he had played poker with back then. Actually, they had taught him how to play. With his buddies in front of him, Jimmy grinned and knew it was going to be a much better day

CHAPTER 7

Waiting and Playing Poker

Meanwhile, back on earth, Maura was waiting to hear back from Bob. She had promised herself to leave him alone to work through his brother's passing. Being kindred spirits, Maura understood the need for space. In her mind, solitude was the only way to handle and process emotional situations. It was opposite the reaction most people had, but that was just one more reason Maura and Bob understood each other on a deeper level.

As Bob's 50th birthday was looming, Maura decided to give in and call him. Bob was very happy to hear from her, and they quickly made a plan to celebrate his big milestone. Maura was busy with a charity event the weekend of Bob's birthday party, so they made plans to get together the following weekend.

Maura got off the phone feeling please that they had made plans and that Bob sounded happier. She thought that maybe things were going better for him overall. While Maura was thinking about her conversation with Bob, Jimmy was watching all of it in the viewing room, even if it was only out of the corner of his eye.

Over the past month, Jimmy had been playing poker nonstop with his war buddies, since Norm had given his okay.

Within a couple of weeks, he had mastered some nuances of the game again—sharpening the skills needed to play a winning poker hand as well as getting a feel for other people's reactions, otherwise known as tells. Jimmy could figure out when they were bluffing based on a hand dealt. He learned quickly that the best way to win at poker was to follow his motto in life, which was always to "look *and be* cool." Thus he found his niche in Heaven-Poker.

Jimmy never gave away the strength of his hand, because he was always acting chill. He found himself looking forward every day to playing poker, because he was completely in his element. Thus he started winning *a lot* of poker games!

Now in Heaven it was obviously much different from earth, and betting for real money was absolutely not allowed. But that didn't mean they couldn't play with real chips; they just weren't able to cash them in. So Jimmy began making major wagers against his pals as each day passed and grew more confident in his poker skills. Every day the pile of chips grew larger on Jimmy's side of the table.

Sometimes Jimmy's war buddies would get pulled away for an angel call and have to leave abruptly. And that's when it became even more interesting for Jimmy because random people would drop in, sit down, and play a few hands with him. Jimmy loved it when this happened, because it tested his abilities and showed how far along he was advancing in the game, especially since he could not read the people very well. As a bonus, he got the opportunity to start meeting other people in heaven.

One day one of his pals suggested that Jimmy play in the major poker tournaments around Heaven. Jimmy didn't even know such events existed, and he was thrilled to partake. He dove in immediately and signed up for two tournaments.

Though he didn't win either, he did very well overall. It didn't matter to him that he didn't win; it was the thrill of knowing that he could hold his own in just a few weeks at tournament level status that had him really excited.

On the day that Maura was to meet Bob to celebrate his birthday, Jimmy sat in the viewing room alone, sulking. He had heard a rumor about a big Poker Tournament that night and that it could turn into a final championship. It was the biggest tournament he knew of so far, with numerous participants who had been playing for several years, but with no final outcome.

Jimmy sighed, thinking about the tournament, knowing he couldn't even be a bystander, never mind a player, because Maura was meeting Bob that night. His obligation was to focus on Maura and Bob from the viewing room, not participate in the Poker Tournament. Jimmy was thrilled to be seeing his brother again, as well as Maura looking so happy, but it was difficult to focus on the upcoming event on earth when all he could think about was the poker game in Heaven.

Maura went shopping during the day to find an outfit that Bob would like. She finally settled on a hot-pink cotton blouse that had a sixties style to it, with flowing long sleeves and a tie at the top of the blouse, which had a circle cut in the middle top part – —showing a hint of her cleavage.

From a distance, Jimmy approved of her choice. Pink was a good color for her, and he wished he could tell her that. Maura had a way of looking classy but sexy when she wanted to, and it was something Jimmy really liked about her—as did Bob. In Maura's mind though her assets were very limited, and she did the best with what she had.

As Maura happily hurried home to get ready for seeing Bob, Jimmy realized there were worse things he could be doing. Who knew—maybe the tournament would really be intense and he would be humiliated, and in addition not get to see his brother. So Jimmy settled in front of the Viewing Room, ready for whatever would happen that night. As he was sitting there, it suddenly dawned on him that, unlike the last time, his sister hadn't appeared to take him down to earth.

"Just one more thing to make the night drag on!" Jimmy mutter out loud with a long sigh.

He missed Pat and wished she would find the time to drop in more often. Speaking of dropping in, Jimmy remembered that he hadn't seen Norm in ages either. Though Norm could be very commanding sometimes and quirky in his own ways, he had grown on Jimmy.

"Who knew?" Jimmy chuckled to himself. He had scarcely seen Norm since he had started playing poker. As a matter of fact, during the few times he dropped in while Jimmy was playing cards with his buddies, the other guys at the table had gotten really quiet—almost like they had gotten caught.

Once, after Norm had quickly left, Jimmy said to one of the other players, "Damn, Norm is a busy little man! What the heck does he do all day?"

His war buddy looked at him strangely and said, "I think that's a question for Norm."

"Why? Do you know him?" Jimmy asked.

His buddy laughed and said, "Everyone knows Norm at some point in their journey here."

Jimmy wasn't sure how to respond to that, so he didn't say anything at the time, but he knew he needed to ask Norm more questions about what he did all day. He thought maybe he could even help Norm out.

With that final thought, he refocused on the viewing screen, wondering how he was going to help Maura if he was in heaven and she was there. At precisely that moment, Norm appeared in the viewing room. Jimmy turned around, stunned to see Norm entering. He said, "I was just thinking about you!"

Norm responded with a gentle smile. "I know, Jimmy. That's why I'm here."

Jimmy leaped up, started pacing around the room, and said excitedly, "Well, Norm, ya know I was thinking, since you seem so busy, and we both know I don't have a lot to do, that I could help you out?"

Norm looked pleased with this, and responded, "Jimmy, I am so impressed with your progress in Heaven! Do you realize what a major step this is for you?"

Jimmy replied, "Huh?"

"You're asking how you can help others. That's what it's all about, my friend. Sadly, you lost track of that on earth."

"That's not true! I certainly helped others in my lifetime."

"Actually, Jimmy, you were more concerned with who was doing what for you in your later years, and it took a toll on those around you." He realized as he spoke that Jimmy was looking perplexed and sullen, so he added, "But enough of dwelling on that for now. We have other things to do."

Jimmy asked, "Like what? Aren't you sending me on an angel adventure down to earth to hang with Maura and Bob?"

Norm replied, "No, I'm going to leave that adventure to your sister, Pat, this time. But I have something for you that I think could be more challenging."

"Really? What would that be?"

"How would you like to play in a Poker Tournament that has been going on and off for over twenty years?"

"Really?! Is that the tournament some people have mentioned recently?"

"Yes, and it's tonight."

"Wow! Cool! I would love to play in it."

Norm said firmly, "Well, I must warn you, it's not your usual stakes."

"You mean not for money? That's okay, Norm. We just play with fake chips anyway."

"Well, that won't be the case this time. You'll be playing with real Roman gold coins."

"OK, that's just fine with me," Jimmy replied with a grin. Then he paused and asked seriously, "But wait, Norm. What about Maura and Bob? How can I be watching them if I'm playing in this big tournament tonight? I thought I was never to let anything take precedence over watching Maura?"

"That's exactly right. Don't worry. There will be a Viewing Room where we're going."

"But won't the other players object, since this is such a serious tournament?"

Norm said with a laugh, "Trust me, my friend, they won't. Okay?" He put his hand on Jimmy's shoulder and gave it a firm, quick squeeze.

Jimmy felt an immediate sense of calm engulf him and responded, "Sure, whatever you say! Lead the way, little man!"

As they started to glide down the hallway, Norm replied, "Oh, now that I'm thinking about it, weren't you looking for these?" He produced Jimmy's sunglasses, which he'd had the night he died on earth.

"My shades!" Jimmy exclaimed happily. "Thanks, man! Now I can go to the tournament looking and being cool."

CHAPTER 8

The Poker Table

Meanwhile, as Norm and Jimmy were gliding, Maura was driving to meet Bob. She had taken extra time and care getting ready, and she felt that she looked good and smelled even better—wearing Bob's favorite perfume of hers, Opium.

As always, she was excited to be seeing him, and that night was to be extra special, since it was his 50th birthday. She had found the perfect card to give him as well as a very special gift. She hoped he would appreciate it as much as she did. Maura was prepared for a great night, with an overnight bag filled with sexy lingerie as well as a bottle of French champagne. Both were in the trunk.

As she pulled into their meeting spot, Maura saw that Bob was already outside of his car and smiling. She stopped the car quickly and leaped into his welcoming arms. She could immediately feel his happiness, and she knew that this night was going to be just fine.

Maura started to get in Bob's car but then realized that her special gifts and bag were in her trunk, so she hesitated. She asked him if they could go back to her car later, after dinner, and he agreed. As they drove off into Boston, they chatted about their day's events. When they arrived in the South End of

Boston to have dinner, they walked along the Wharf to a very cool seafood restaurant called The Barking Crab. In all the years it had existed, Maura had never been there, but it was Bob's pick for a place to eat, and a good one! Without discussing it, they simultaneously ordered the same food off the menu: Lobster.

As Maura sat waiting for her beer, she reflected on how unique their relationship was. Some couples that had been together for years would argue about where they were going, why they were going there, and what the plan was after that. Bob and Maura just believed in being in the moment, in a place, with each other. They were so happy when they were together that details of where, when, and why were just irrelevant.

Maura looked over at Bob and smiled. She starting telling him how she swore she'd seen a UFO in a field that day. And if on cue, the bartender asked, "Would you like our draft beer of the night from UFO Brewery?"

Bob looked at her in disbelief, and Maura just smiled, laughed, and said, "It's going to be a magical night!"

At that exact moment, back in Heaven, Norm stopped in front of an ordinary-looking viewing room and gestured for Jimmy to enter. Jimmy walked into the room where the Poker Championship was to be played and immediately encountered a room full of people arguing and pointing at the viewing screen showing Maura and Bob at the bar of the restaurant.

Someone was talking over the others, saying, "Oh come on! You believe her? She did *not* see a UFO today. They don't exist!"

And Jimmy looked over across the room, he even saw a favorite uncle from his past arguing with another. "Her description of the UFO wasn't even right!"

"How would you know? Have you ever even seen one?"

"No—have you?"

"Oy Vey!" Jimmy mumbled and turned to Norm, who was

observing the mayhem as well. Norm sighed heavily, stepped into the room, and said in a loud firm voice, "People, pipe down for a minute! I need your attention."

Everyone turned toward the entryway and stopped midsentence whatever they were saying, and within seconds there was silence in the room. Jimmy found this to be very impressive. As he observed the room, he noticed that everyone looked stunned to see them. It made Jimmy proud to be standing next to Norm. Obviously he was an Angel VIP of some sort.

Norm smiled gently and said to everyone in the room, "Ah, that's much better. Now I would like to introduce to you a stellar poker player who will be joining the tournament game tonight: Jimmy, -Level 1 Angel. What is most impressive about Jimmy is that he's been in Heaven only a short while, but in that time he has become very successful at his assignment—and, I might add, his poker game. So I expect you all to give him the respect he deserves, and may he present a challenge to you all!"

Norm looked at one table in particular and continued. "In case some of you were not aware, Jimmy has been assigned as a spirit guide angel to Maura. I know that some of you in this room have been watching over Maura at a higher level for years, but Jimmy brings a special element to the task at hand. He is Bob's brother. Thus I expect you all to welcome Jimmy in as one of Maura's guardians." Everyone at that particular table nodded in unison, but in silence.

With this Norm turned to Jimmy and said, "Now I need to place you at the table closest to the viewing screen. Based on this, I believe you should sit at the front table." Jimmy observed there were four tables all together, but he started walking to where Norm had suggested. All of a sudden, Jimmy looked over at the most distant table, and as he thought earlier, there sitting at the table was his favorite Uncle Joey.

Jimmy stopped, turned around, and said, "Hey, wait a second, Norm. Let me sit at the table with Uncle Joey, so we can get caught up on old times."

Norm replied firmly, "He is here only to make the game more interesting. You need to be at the front table with Maura's relatives."

Jimmy sighed aloud and slowly scuffed his way over to the front table with a sullen look on his face. He didn't like it at all. The table was all women—older, wiser women, truth be told—and he wasn't sure how he felt about playing poker with them. Furthermore, Jimmy wondered why there was a room full of Maura's and Bob's relatives for the Poker Championship.

Jimmy turned back to Norm and said in a quiet voice, "I don't get it. I thought this was the *BIG* Poker Tournament, and yet now you have me hanging out with the relatives? What's up with that?"

Norm patiently said, "Jimmy I told you on the glide over here that this is no ordinary poker tournament or stakes. I think it will become clear to you as the game progresses tonight what the bet is."

Norm quickly turned and walked towards the doorway, and then said, "I have other pressing matters to attend to, but I have one last piece of advice for you, Jimmy, before I leave. Keep the sunglasses on that I gave you earlier. I know how sensitive you still are to the light, and there is plenty of that in this room." With that, Norm smiled at the women at the first table, quickly turned, and was gone.

Collectively there was a sigh of relief from people in the room. One murmured, "Wow, I can't believe he came to visit us!" Jimmy could tell he definitely had been hanging with a VIP in heaven.

Jimmy stared at the table that he had been assigned to, and

he realized that all six seats were taken, so he slowly started to back away and edge over toward his Uncle Joey's table. He wasn't counting on the fact that the eldest angel at his table didn't miss a thing. She turned quickly toward him and said like a schoolteacher, "Oh, Jimmy, where do you think you're going?"

"Well, there doesn't seem to be enough room at your table." The elder angel with beautiful long silver hair replied, "Well, give me a minute, and I'll make room!" She turned quickly and said, "Helen, you're out! You're not that great of a poker player, and besides, you're too slow. We appreciate your interest and concern for Maura, but you're going to have to pass on this tournament."

Helen said quietly, "Okay, E. B., I understand." And without any further argument or protest, she got up quickly to leave the room. Personally Jimmy was stunned by her action and found the dialogue annoying, and a put-down to Helen. *Who does this E. B. woman think she is?* Jimmy wondered. *She doesn't own the table!*

Just as he was thinking this, another taller elder angel stood up and said, "Oh, Eleanor, you know that the worst player at the table is *me*. Therefore Jimmy can have my seat, and Helen can continue to play. You know how much she loves the game."

The elder angel snapped firmly, "Sit down, Jenny! You know how much I need you at the table tonight. It's too important for you to be anywhere else but here."

As he watched the verbal exchange, Jimmy thought, *I don't even want to be at this woman's table!*

The elder angel, Eleanor, whose long, silver hair glistened beautiful in the light, turned her attention to Jimmy. He was for once very happy to be an angel, because if he was in human form, he would have felt stripped naked under her intense stare and stern assessment. "Well then," she said, "we don't have all night, Jimmy. Please come sit down!" He quickly did just that. The angel started shuffling the deck of cards and then stared at him intently again. "Do you have any idea who I am?" she asked proudly.

Jimmy resisted rolling his eyes and just said, "No, ma'am, I do not." He was instantly annoyed with himself that he called her *ma'am*.

"I'm Maura's grandmother, otherwise known as her Nana." Then she added quite proudly with a bit of a haughty look at Jimmy, "I am also the eldest angel at the table."

Jimmy nodded toward her and said, "It's very nice to meet you. I read about you in Maura's file." He bit his tongue from adding how much it seemed that Maura worshipped the woman. *What's the point? Eleanor already acts like she's quite aware of this,* Jimmy thought.

To his right at the poker table was a tall elder angel. She tugged gently at his angel robe, and when he turned to her, she softly said, "I'm Jenny, Maura's other grandmother. Eleanor will tell you that she is the only Nana Maura remembers, but that's not true! She loved us both—very much. I just didn't last on earth as long as the Energizer Bunny over there did—, otherwise known as E. B. for short—so she likes to take all the credit." Jenny gave a quick smile and then added, "But enough about that. Let's introduce you to the rest of the gang at the poker table." Jimmy met another aunt, and while Jenny was talking, another person appeared at the table, a man, known as Edwin, who was Eleanor's brother.

Just as Jimmy was shaking Edwin's hand, all of a sudden he heard Uncle Joey at the other table shout, "Hey, Jimmy, I haven't seen you in years! Come say hello to your favorite uncle!" So Jimmy quickly went over to his table, and as soon as he got there, Uncle Joey grabbed him in a bear hug and whispered in his ear, "She's gonna kick your butt!" Jimmy moved back and stared at him incredulously and said, "Who?"

Uncle Joey gestured with a nod of his head to the poker table in the front of the viewing room and said in a low voice, "The Energizer Bunny over there. She's been playing cards for years. Don't let her seniority fool you. They don't call her E. B. for short for nothing, kiddo."

Jimmy said, "Hey, come on, Uncle Joey! Have some faith in the family. I'll hold my own just fine against the old biddy."

"Don't be so sure, son. Edwin isn't sittin' at the table just to be around a bunch of elder female angels. He is her sidekick in the game. They play off each other and with a total code list of tells."

"Well, Uncle Joey, I'm not too concerned—so don't you be." With that, Jimmy walked back to his chair.

By this point, Eleanor—a.k.a. E. B.—had finished shuffling the deck of cards and was intently looking at the viewing screen, which was showing Bob and Maura still having dinner at The Barking Crab. Bob was sharing a story with Maura, and she was laughing and smiling.

E. B. turned to Jenny and said, "I have a good feeling about tonight."

Jenny replied with hope in her voice "You do, E. B.? Really? I know I've said that so many times before over the last twenty years, but I have always been wrong in the end. So I've just stopped saying it out loud, even though I have never stopped praying and believing."

"I know, Jenny," E. B. said and gently patted her hand. "Something tells me that tonight is different; it could finally be the real thing."

"I *so* hope you're right. No one has a bigger heart full of love than Maura, and I hope Bob sees that and doesn't run away from her because it's too overwhelming a commitment."

And with that said, E. B. addressed the table. "Let the Poker Championship game begin. The bet, as always, is "Winning Maura's Heart."

CHAPTER 9

The Birthday Celebration

As the Championship Poker game was starting, all eyes in the room were on the viewing screen, which was showing Maura and Bob wrapping up their dinner.

Maura was having a great time. She loved the quirky New England restaurant that resided along the wharf in Boston. She and Bob had gotten to know the couple next to them at the bar, and Bob had the delightful experience of learning how to open a lobster claw with a rock. *Only a man would find this to be the highlight of his dinner,* Maura mused. As the night went on, she hated to leave, but she knew Bob was ready to go. The night was still young in his eyes—so off they went.

Since it was a gorgeous, warm fall night, they walked around the wharf and took in the beautiful Boston skyline with its diverse architecture. The full moon only added to the night, illuminating some of the most unique and old structures in Boston. More importantly, it was romantic and thus a perfect night to take a stroll through the city.

Eventually they reached Bob's car, and he drove them back to their earlier meeting place. Maura was happy she had made him agree ahead of time to this plan. She could tell that he was in a jovial mood, having drunk a good amount at the bar, and she didn't want him to become concerned about driving later in the night.

Once they settled into her car, they had to decide where to go. Maura was determined to make it a romantic location. They could have gone back to her place or even gotten a room at a B&B somewhere, but to Maura that was just ordinary. In her mind, turning 50 was no ordinary event. *Besides,* she thought, *it is probably one of the last Indian Summer nights left of the fall, so why spend it inside?*

As Maura sat in the car, listening to Bob suggesting various spots or places to hang out, it hit her where the perfect location would be. Maura turned and said excitedly with a gleaming smile, "OK Bob, I know the perfect spot to go. Trust me!"

Bob looked at her and saw her blue Irish eyes sparkling, and he couldn't help but smile. "Okay, kiddo, lead the way!" Then he leaned over and gave her a passionate kiss as she put the car in reverse.

They chatted up a storm as Maura drove into the suburbs outside Boston. They didn't bring up Jimmy, and that was just fine with Maura, since she didn't want anything to bring down the mood of the night and Bob's high spirits. Maura realized as their cheery banter was taking place that she could never stay mad at Bob. It truly was impossible; as soon as she saw him, all her anxiety or annoyance with him just melted away, and she realized it was trivial in the grand scheme of things in life. Their relationship was too deep and special to focus on the negative.

As they got closer to the special location that Maura had picked, she took a bunch of country back roads to disorient Bob.

When Maura finally pulled into the wooded area across from the surprise location, she knew she had succeeded in surprising him, because Bob looked totally perplexed as to where they were. She got out of the car and again went to the trunk. She called out to Bob for help, and he came around to the back of the car. She thrust a huge blanket into his arms as well as a flashlight, then said, "Don't lose the flashlight, or we're screwed!" She then grabbed the present, the card, and the bottle of French champagne, and said, "Okay then, let's go!"

Bob said, "Hang on, Maura. Where we are going?"

She smiled mischievously and said, "Well, Bob, why don't you at least get us across the street safely first, and then the mysterious location will reveal itself slowly to you."

Bob started leading the way with the flashlight, through the dark parking lot, and across a country road, which usually was totally dark at that time of night. Once they got across the street, Maura couldn't contain her excitement. She loved this place and gasped as Walden Pond came into view when they reached the surrounding woods.

Below them unfolded a beautiful large pond with the full moon shining down on its calm water. It was surrounded by woods wherever you looked. There had been many articles written about the wonders of the world, and Maura had always felt that Walden Pond should be on the list, but it never was.

It was the location where Henry David Thoreau built a cabin and wrote his books on nature and life. Walden Pond was magical, and Maura could feel it each time she went there. She could feel it in the earth, the air, and the calmness and serenity of the water engulfed by the surrounding woods.

THIS was the place that Maura had picked to bring Bob for the Celebration Finale of his 50th birthday. They walked down the long, steep pathway to the pond in silence. When they finally reached the pond, Bob stopped and said, "Wow! How did you know to bring me here?"

Maura replied, "It seemed the perfect night to come here. But I never knew you had been here before. When?"

Bob looked at her intently with eyes that seemed to gleam in the reflection of the light of the moon off the water. "I use to come here years ago, all the time, with my brother Jimmy. He loved this place."

Before Maura could stop herself, she shouted, "What?" which echoed around the pond.

Bob looked at her in surprise and shook his head. "You're amazing. Of all the places we could have gone, and yet you brought me here, where I have so many special memories. My brother and I had some really good times at Walden Pond." He paused and turned away, blinking.

Meanwhile Maura was thinking, *Damn that man! Here I was trying to plan a happy, peaceful night and without asking me, he somehow becomes the highlight of conversation and could turn the evening into a total buzz kill!* Maura firmly decided in her mind that she was not going to dwell on Jimmy and let him or his spirit ruin the night. She abruptly turned away from Bob, and as she started to walk ahead, she said, "Well, that's me for ya, Bob! Let's find a good spot to sit down and take in the beautiful scenery."

Maura continued walking until she found a secluded area near the pond with sand but far enough away from the main road and entrance area. The last thing she wanted was to be discovered by the wandering town cops or other freaky people. She waited for Bob to catch up and said, "OK, this looks perfect to me. Let's spread out the blanket and shut off the flashlight, since the moon is providing all the illumination we need for now."

Once they were settled and comfy in the dark, Maura pulled out the champagne she had brought as well as the card and present. She opened up the bottle of champagne, cuddled up to Bob, and said, "I have something special for your birthday, but I want you to read the card first."

Bob rolled his eyes in response. "I forgot my glasses. You're gonna have to read the card to me, hon."

Maura smiled and said softly, "I don't mind doing that at all." She pulled out the card, and while leaning on his broad shoulder, she described the card—how it had an antique pocket watch on the front with the words on the cover "As time goes by." Inside were the words "always remember to live life to the fullest—in every moment."

Then Maura read what she had written on the inside of the card for him,. "Ever since I met you, when I was only 18, one of the most important things you said to me was to live for the moment. It's a message I have carried within me since then. In many cases, it's what has gotten me through so much over the years—remembering to focus on those precious moments I had captured. It was one of life's most important messages, but not many people had taken the time to master it like you had."

Maura continued to read, telling him not to dwell on the past. "Let those that had died rest in peace." (At this point she went into a coughing fit.) Once she had recovered, she read on and told Bob that he needed to focus on the future and on the wonderful events and moments that would unfold and be shared with others—like her.

When Maura finished and looked up from the card, Bob's eyes were glistening again, and without saying a word, he pulled her into his arms and said into her ear, "That was the most beautiful card and note that anyone has ever written to me." Then he slowly kissed her.

Maura ran her hand over his handsome face, looked into his kind brown eyes, and said, "But wait! There's more. I haven't given you your gift yet." Smiling, Maura pulled away and reached for the French Champagne. Then she pulled out a velvet pouch she had in a beach bag, and she asked him to open it. Bob pushed open the drawstrings and pulled out two wrapped items, which he carefully unwrap, revealing two fluted champagne glasses. Maura filled both of the glasses with champagne and handed one to him. Bob looked at his glass and then over at Maura, mystified. He could see she was watching him intently.

Maura said, "You have no idea how upset I was earlier today when I found only one of this pair. I ripped apart my house looking for the other glass. Luckily I found it. You don't know where these plain fluted glasses are from, do you?"

Bob replied quietly, "No, I'm sorry I don't. Why don't you tell me?"

"These champagne glasses are from the first New Year's we spent together—and it's the first keepsake I still have from our time together over twenty years ago. These glasses have survived all my moves, all my changes in taste, and all my failures and successes. I could afford Waterford glasses now, but the plain, ordinary fluted glasses are worth one hundred thousand times the value to me, because they represent you, all our good times together, and my love for you, then and now. I could never part with these two glasses. It's as if *I knew* I would see you again and use them. What better time than tonight?"

By this point, Maura was too overwhelmed and choked up to say anything else. She also was waiting for Bob's reaction. He looked at her, and she could see tears in his eyes. He put his glass down in the sand and took her face delicately in his hands, stared deeply into her eyes, and said what she had been waiting to her all her life from him. "I love you, Maura. I always have. I don't say that lightly. You know that. You are the most remarkable woman I have ever known. You are so brave, so strong to overcome everything that you have in life, and yet here you are with me after all these years." Then he looked away and out at the pond, with the moon shining down, and murmured, "What's my problem? What the hell am I waiting for?"

He then turned back to her and said, "I should have asked you to married me the first night we reconnected last year. Maura, you and I should just go to Vegas and get married—like right now. Let's not waste any more time."

Maura was too stunned to speak. Finally she found her voice, "We can't do that, Bob. The last flight already left tonight." And with that, she added with a smile, "But there's always tomorrow."

Bob burst out laughing, pulled her back into his arms, and started passionately kissing her. As Maura pulled away to catch her breath, she started to say, "I love you too!" but Bob cut her off. "Let me show you how much I love you," he said. And then he turned and pulled her onto the blanket with him. Maura was pretty overwhelmed by that point, so she actually sat up and said, "Gee, Bob! We're missing out on the beautiful view the pond and moon are giving us, as well as the rest of the champagne,"

Bob replied, "I would have to agree with you. Let's have another glass and toast to us—our past and our future." He poured them each another glass. Maura sipped slowly at her champagne and looked out over the serene pond. She instinctively wanted to say, "Hang on, Bob. Let me think this through for a minute." But as she looked over at him, she realized he was drinking the champagne much quicker than she, as if it was beer. But she decided not to say anything, lest it destroy the loving atmosphere surrounding her.

Instead Maura lay back, breathed in deeply, let out a big

sigh, turned to Bob, and said "I want you to make love to me here—at Walden Pond—tonight. It's just too magical a night not too."

Bob softly replied, "How could I not make love to you here tonight? There is no other place I would want to be." He pulled her back into his arms.

As things started to passionately progress and clothes were quickly coming off, Maura had two distinct fears: of wild nocturnal animals in the woods wandering by for a sniff—or a chew—during the night and the fear that local cops would discover them buck naked at Walden Pond. There was no telling what the charge and fine would be for that.

Maura started to slow things down in protest and brought up those gnawing but important concerns to Bob as he was unhooking her bra. Without hesitation, he replied with a classic response: "Live for the moment, Maura."

With that, she let herself be engulfed by his slow, sensuous touch. They made love on the sand with a level of emotional intensity they hadn't experienced before. Luckily, during their passionate lovemaking, the cops did not show up—if they had, Maura and Bob would have never know.

Afterward, Maura lay in Bob's arms, staring out at the pond. She pulled the big blanket up and wrapped it around both of them to keep warm and to keep from being exposed to any unwanted visitors.

As she went to lean on Bob's shoulder, Maura stopped and noticed from the moonlight that there was a bug on his shoulder. She went to flick it off, and then suddenly stopped short. "Bob," she said, "you're not going to believe this: ... but you have a ladybug on your shoulder! I guess it was your lucky night, honey." And then, with a contented smile, she snuggled up to him, closed her eyes, and whispered, "Wake me when it's light out, Bob." With those words, she quickly fell asleep.

Meanwhile, Bob was lying in the sand with his head spinning and his stomach rolling. He realized too late that he'd had too much to drink and that beer and champagne do not mix. All of a sudden, he leaped up, causing the ladybug to fly off his shoulder, and dashed into the woods to get sick. He stayed there for a while until he was certain his stomach had settled down. During his misery, he failed to notice the ladybug take flight above him and turn into an angel with huge beautiful wings as she reached the stars.

Bob slowly went back to the sand, lay down on the blanket, and saw to his relief that Maura was still asleep. He stared at her Irish face in the moonlight and thought, *What an amazing night.* And with that he passed out.

Pat hovered high in the night sky, watching Bob. If he had looked straight up in the sky, he would have seen a brightly lit star. With distress on her face and her wings fluttering in anxiousness, Pat quietly said over and over, "No! No, Bob! Please don't black out!" But as hard as she tried to wish it different, her wish didn't happen. Her worst fear of the night was realized: Bob would not remember the incredible night when he woke up.

With that, Pat spread her wings out as far as they would go and frantically took off toward heaven to warn Jimmy of what was to come.

CHAPTER 10

The Championship Game

While Maura and Bob were at Walden Pond, back up in Heaven, Jimmy was playing the most challenging poker game of his eternal life.

Damn, this woman EB was really good! he thought. Each time he had her figured out, Edwin would jump in, play a hand, and throw a wrench in any progress Jimmy had been making in the game. He couldn't figure out any of E. B. and Edwin's tells, because they kept switching things up. It was as if E. B. was saying, "Come on, big shot, show me what you've got!"

Needless to say, she was really starting to annoy him. The only bright light, literally, at the table was Jenny, and Jimmy was glad to have her at his side. In her motherly, celestial way, she calmed him down. She whispered words of encouragement each time he lost a hand, which was often, so truth be told, he needed it. E. B. was unnerving him. Had he been in human form, he'd be sweating profusely by then.

In addition, because of the pressure, Jimmy found himself craving a Martini in the worst way. "How is this even possible? I'm dead, right?" he mumbled to himself.

Jimmy had stopped keeping his eyes on the viewing screen to see what was going on at Walden Pond. The last time he had glanced up, they had just arrived there. As Jimmy looked at his dwindling pile of poker chips, he realized that taking a break was absolutely needed. He got up from the table, and stated, "Ladies, and Edwin, I need to take a break for a few hands. Please continue playing. Consider me on pass for now, and knock yourselves out while I'm gone."

With that Jimmy quickly went over to Uncle Joey's table and murmured, "Take a break with me now." Uncle Joey looked a bit taken aback, but got up and said, "Okay, Jimmy. Sure," and told his table he'd pass on a few hands.

Outside in the cloud hallway, Jimmy started to pace up and down the corridor. Uncle Joey watched in amusement and said, "What's got you SO fired up? Didn't I warn you about E. B.?"

Jimmy whipped around quickly, stopped in front of him, and said "It's *SO* intense in there! And E. B.—" He stopped, at a loss for words. "Man, it's like she can predict or see through my cards or something. What am I gonna do now? She's about to shut me down—and damn it, I need a drink!"

Uncle Joey burst out into a loud, deep laugh, and said, "Sorry, buddy, but it's a dry town up here."

"I'm aware of that, but it doesn't help to be reminded at the moment," Jimmy snapped. "Besides, I have more important things to worry about, like how am I going to survive in this tournament, against E. B. and Edwin, never mind win?"

Uncle Joey said, "Look, I used to crave cigars something fierce when I first came up here. But trust me, the cravings fade over time." He started to pace the hallway, in deep thought. Finally he stopped, turned back toward Jimmy, and said seriously, "There is only one solution if you're going to win this championship."

"What's that?"

"You have to go *ALL IN* when you're back at the table and

get dealt the next hand. You only have two more hands left anyway, so you don't have a choice."

Jimmy looked at him incredulously and said, "Are you nuts? ALL IN? I can't believe you're even suggesting this. I'll be out of the game in the next five minutes—or less. No way, Uncle Joey."

Uncle Joey walked closer and stared him in the face. "Look at me. Trust me, Jimmy! They won't expect it from you. That's the beauty of making this move," he said excitedly. "E. B. will never believe you have the guts to do it. Prove her wrong. Your move will throw her and Edwin way off, and that's what you need to keep in the game."

Jimmy looked at him warily. Uncle Joey took that as a good sign and continued. "You need to stay in this game; it's too important. Why else would Norm have brought you here? It's not just about the championship, Jimmy. It's about the outcome tonight down on earth more than here in that room. And you hold the opposing view to everyone else at that table! You and I both know that Bob will never pull the trigger and ask Maura to marry him. The bet tonight was that he will ask her, but you know better. And besides *if* you win the Poker championship bet, you take home all the Roman coins. And that earns you respect in heaven, even though you can't buy things."

Jimmy murmured, "The Roman coins are kinda cool."

With that, before Jimmy could object further, Uncle Joey walked him to the Poker Room entrance, pulled back the door, and said, "Get back in there and go all in. Make the family proud, Jimmy! I totally believe in you, buddy. You know that." And with that, he gave him a big smile and a bowing gesture at the door.

Jimmy hesitated at the entrance. Then he felt the love emanating from his favorite uncle, so he slowly grinned and said, "Okay, I'll do it. I'm all in!" With that he stepped back into the room, ready for more poker action.

"That's my boy!" Uncle Joey exclaimed from the hallway.

Jimmy quickly sat down at his table with an air of confidence and determination that hadn't been there before. He glanced at the viewing screen to see that Bob and Maura were settling in at Walden's beach. Then he looked around the table, and said, "I'm ready now. Hit me." E. B. dealt a new hand of cards.

Thus began a new poker game and strategy by Jimmy. The hand that was dealt was a good one for him, a pair of Jacks. Edwin called, Jimmy matched him, and as each person around the table stated his or her position and all cards were dealt, it was time to turn over the final cards on the river. At that point, Jimmy said, "I'm all in."

Watching everyone's reaction was priceless. Jenny gasped, Edwin had a coughing fit, and E. B. looked stunned and said, "I beg your pardon?"

Jimmy repeated his call then sat and waited on E. B. She sighed loudly and in a huff said, "Alrighty then. I'm all in too." She put her hands under her chin, stared at Jimmy, glanced slightly to her right, and said, "Edwin?" Edwin was silent for a minute, pondering the situation, cleared his throat, and finally said, "Um, I'll pass."

Jimmy did everything he could do not to fist pump the heavenly clouds and scream, "*Yes!*" He tried to contain himself somehow. He had found his ace in the hole; Uncle Joey had been SO right. Edwin didn't have the guts to go all in, and thus E. B. didn't have her sidekick. It was a critical turning point in the game.

The poker game proceeded, and when all cards on the table had been turned over, Jimmy ended up winning over E. B. with his pair of Jacks. It was a beautiful sight to see the Roman coins coming across the table from E. B.'s pile to Jimmy's side. He couldn't help but turn and sneak a big fat grin at Uncle Joey.

What a great uncle, he thought. *His advice had always been wise, and in heaven it's the best.*

With each game onward, he started winning big with his new strategy, and the coins started piling up. Eventually Edwin folded for good, and Jenny was much more focused on the happenings at Walden Pond than the poker game. In Jimmy's eyes, that was a very good thing, because he had been laser focused on the game, and winning instead. As he was taking the game more seriously, he noticed that Jenny, in her cool angelic way, had her hands folded in her lap and was praying while watching things unfold at Walden.

All of a sudden, in the middle of a hand being dealt, Jenny exclaimed, "E. B., look at what's happening at Walden. I *told you* I had a great feeling about tonight, and I was right!" Then she clapped her hands in ecstatic happiness.

E. B. put her cards down and focused on the screen to see Bob proposing to Maura on the sand. "Well, I'll be damned. Who knew? It's about time. I am so happy for her." Jenny leaped up, and went over to hug her, and started to cry.

E. B. looked over her shoulder at Jimmy. "Looks like your brother finally came through."

Jimmy, on the other hand, was too shocked to respond. He was trying to figure out what was going on. He had missed the whole event leading up to the proposal. He looked at the screen and then at Jenny, and said "Wait, how did I miss this? Bob proposing to Maura? Are you sure? That can't be happening."

Jenny said with a huge smile on her face, "Well, yes, it is!"

Jimmy looked concerned as his viewed the screen and scene below. "Honestly, ladies, my brother is the most commitment phobic person I know. He got really burnt the first time around and vowed he'd never marry again—to his whole family. So I just can't believe this just took place."

Jenny turned to him and said, "Noooo, please don't say that, Jimmy. Everyone has a change of heart over time, and Maura must have softened his. All I know is that Maura loves him deeply, and why doesn't she deserve that in return?"

"Look, I don't want to be the buzz kill for the happiness vibe you've got going on here. I'm just saying I know my brother well, and this is not what I would have expected—ever," Jimmy stated seriously.

E. B. jumped in finally, saying in a clipped tone, "Well, you're wrong! And besides, the bet tonight was for whether Bob would finally propose to Maura—*and he did*. So I win the pile of coins." She started to reach for Jimmy's pile.

Jimmy exclaimed, "Whoa! Hold on, Ms. Energizer Bunny! What the heck are you talking about? The championship is based on poker card playing skills, not on some made-up wish or bet before the game started."

E. B. replied, "Sorry, buster, but you didn't pay attention. Must not have good listening skills."

Jenny stood up, looked at both of them with distain, and said, "Both of you, stop! This is ridiculous—it's just a silly game. And you're losing sight of the most important outcome of this event: That Maura is truly loved and is getting married to her soulmate."

Jimmy replied, "Jenny, as much as I really like hanging out with you and love your cool vibe, I have to disagree on your point. It is about the poker game championship, and based on how many hands I won consistently tonight, I've earned the entire pot of coins."

E. B. whipped around and stared at Edwin, who had wisely kept out of the discussion so far. "Edwin, help me out here. I think the answer and outcome is quite clear. Agree?

Edwin pondered this for about thirty seconds and said,

"E. B., keep me out of this. I've been out of the game for many hands tonight."

"*Fine*, then I will take matters into my own hands." E. B. quickly reached across the table to grab all of Jimmy's coins.

Just then the door flung open wide, and Pat came rushing across the room to Jimmy. "I need you now, so please come outside with me," she said.

He glanced up from the table, hovering over his coins, and said, "Kinda busy right now, Pat. What's up?"

Jenny could see the stress on Pat's face and said, "Hey, honey, what's wrong? You look really upset."

Pat replied, "I am. Weren't you all watching? Or were you too caught up in your stupid poker game to see?"

Jimmy mumbled, "Um, yeah, I think so." But he was starting to realize that no one, except Jenny, had been watching the TV. They had been playing poker and arguing about the Roman Coins instead.

Pat replied firmly, "Outside, Jimmy."

He said, "Look, sis. I'm really trying to wrap up this poker game here with E. B., and we're in a dispute over which of us gets the Coins. Can't it wait?"

As Pat began to open her mouth to snap back a reply, all of a sudden the room boomed with a loud voice that said, "Enough!" It was like a clap of thunder reverberating off the walls. Everyone stopped and stood frozen in their spot as the booming voice continued: "This poker game is over. All poker games will be stopped for now." Then there was complete silence.

Jenny whispered to E. B., "Now we've done it, Eleanor. That never happens!"

E. B. replied quietly, "Hush, Jenny."

Pat looked over again at Jimmy and said, "*Now* will you go

outside with me?" He got up quickly and started following her out of the room, but not without staring at E. B. first.

Once outside in the hallway, Jimmy sighed and said, "Geez, I just wanted to play a good game of poker tonight. What's up with all the drama? And why are you looking so stressed out, Pat?"

With a concerned look, she said, "Bob blacked out down there. He had too much to drink."

Jimmy shrugged. "So, it happens."

Pat snapped quickly "You really weren't watching, were you? Damn it, Jimmy—that's your *job*!"

"Okay, calm down, sis. It's not the end of the world as we know it."

"Jimmy, he won't remember any of it—zip, nada, nothing—when he wakes up."

"Let me get this straight: Bob proposed—which I still can't get my head wrapped around—got a yes, drank a lot in celebration, and then blacked out to a point that when he wakes up in the morning, he won't remember any of it?"

"Exactly. And you know what's even worse? Maura fell asleep thinking she was finally engaged to the man she loves."

"Wow. Okay then." Jimmy saw the grave concern in Pat's eyes. He added, "Damn, our brother is a piece of work," and started to pace the hallway.

Pat walked by his side and added, "We both know Bob's going to wake up and deny it. And then tell her no way, that he won't go through with it. Jimmy, do you realize what that means and how serious this is? The absolute worst part is what this will do to Maura. She's going to be totally devastated."

Jimmy stopped pacing and asked, "Can we bring in an angel intervention from Jenny or something?"

"No, Jimmy, it's all on you now. THIS is why you've been

assigned to protect Maura. We both need to go back down to Walden Pond together, before the sun comes up, so we're at their sides when they wake up. Me for Bob, you for Maura."

"Okay then, let's go now," Jimmy said anxiously.

Quickly Pat brought him over to a spot where she knew they could take the slide down quickly. As they went down, with Jimmy hanging onto Pat, it reminded him of all the fun times they had sledding when they were kids. When they arrived at Walden, it was still dark, and they hung out nearby while Bob and Maura were sleeping, waiting for dawn to arrive.

Meanwhile, back at the Poker Room, things quickly wrapped up. Everyone started going back to their cloud cubes. Uncle Joey announced that he would work on trying to get poker games reinstated. E. B. and Jenny quietly left and made their way back slowly to their respective cloud levels. Both were pensive and somber as they glided along together.

Finally Jenny said, "Eleanor, we lost focus tonight on our purpose here in Heaven. It's never been about a poker game or Roman coins. It's all above *love* and protecting those we love on earth. You know this!"

"I know, Jenny. I'm so sorry I let a poker game get out of hand. And who knows if we'll ever be able to play again, after tonight's antics."

"That doesn't matter now. What is of most importance is to protect Maura, as we always have done. You saw Pat's face tonight. Something went wrong; I can feel it. I'm going to go to the prayer room now to pray hard for her and Bob." She paused. "And E. B., you need to find a way to help too. You are such a powerful and wise angel. Use your gift toward this! Maura is going to need your help, even though we don't know what happened."

E. B. turned, smiled at her, and said, "You are the most caring angel I know, and we'll all be in good hands with you praying. I don't know how a wonderful event like getting engaged tonight would take a turn in the wrong direction, but I'm sure we'll both find out soon enough."

At this point, they reached a fork in the cloud levels, and Jenny said, "E. B., go snooze-doze for a bit. You will need it so you have plenty of energy later if you're called on." With that she rose up toward the higher level with her beautiful golden wings glistening and blew a kiss to E. B.

E. B. basked in her incredible warm light and love as Jenny rose up higher to the level 11 floor. E. B. sighed and thought, *She is always in a calm state of grace, and I'm always ready to defend those I love and get into arguments with people. But that's why she's at a higher level than me.* With that, E. B. glided to her cloud cube, which she considered home now.

When she got there, a lovable Sheltie named Lad was there to greet her. He liked hanging out in E. B.'s cloud cube, and that night E. B. couldn't get enough love from him as he barked and ran around in circles at her feet. Finally he calmed down, and E. B. crumpled into her comfy cloud bed and immediately dozed off, with Lad on the floor nearby.

Sometime later, she opened her eyes because she sensed a warm glow in her room. When she looked at the foot of the bed, there was Norm, gently smiling at her. "Norm! Is something wrong? Has a tragic event happened or something? I'm sorry I was snooze-dozing."

"No, E. B., luckily no bad events. I just decided to visit and talk with you."

"Norm, if this is about the poker game, I am so sorry I let it get out of hand. I should have never acted the way I did to Jimmy and everyone else at the table and in the room."

Norm shook his head and said, "Well, you did lose focus, but then again, so did Jimmy. And that's why I decided to pair both of you to help Maura and Bob. I'm not sure if you're aware of the situation, but Maura is going to wake up soon, and everything is going to spiral out of control very quickly when she realizes that Bob doesn't recall proposing to her last night. He's not going to remember any of it, except maybe arriving at Walden. And he's going to deny proposing to her."

E. B. gasped. "No way! That's just awful, Norm. Why would he take it back? *Why?* He loves her!"

"We would all hope so, but in the meantime, I need your help to look after Maura."

"Always, you know that, Norm," she stated quickly.

"You need to join Jimmy and Pat down at Walden Pond now before daylight hits. And you need to get along with Jimmy. Understood? This situation needs both of you working together to help Maura through this."

"I'll do my best. But what if another tragedy strikes while I'm handling this?"

Norm smiled at her concern. "E. B., you've built an amazing team of angels beneath you. They can handle things if needed. I need your total focus on Maura—to make sure a tragedy doesn't happen with her."

"Absolutely! I would hope that Maura wouldn't do anything stupid because of Bob."

"Ahhh, Bob sadly just doesn't know how to deal with things in the right way. He didn't read the instruction manual on relationships and marriage," Norm said with a sigh.

"Okay, Norm. I'll head down there right away."

"Great, I'm counting on you!"

"Always," E. B. said with a smile. With that, she got ready to fly down to Walden, and Norm said a prayer and gave her a blessing as he watched her leave.

CHAPTER 11

Meanwhile, Back at Walden

As E. B. arrived at Walden Pond and joined Pat and Jimmy along the stonewall steps near the trail around the pond, dawn was just starting to break. As they looked across the pond, it was a breathtaking moment and view. The water, trees, and nature overall were completely still, as if just waiting for the day to begin.

The three angels sat in silence, taking in the beauty and magic of the moment. Eventually E. B. turned to Jimmy and broke the silence. "Norm sent me down and asked that we work together side by side to help Maura through whatever unfolds today." Jimmy just nodded as he looked seriously at his brother and Maura, who were still sleeping, curled up together on the sand. He was anxious about what was about to happen and how the day would evolve.

He also knew that having E. B. join him was either going to make or break his day. But as his sat there pondering the situation, he realized that if Norm sent her, there had to be a good reason. Besides, E. B. and Maura had been very close on earth, and Jimmy didn't have that history. And so he really didn't mind having E. B. joining to help out. He was actually feeling a bit over his head with the intensity of the situation overall.

Before E. B. showed up, Pat had had a chat with him, telling him to respect E. B., because she had a lot of responsibility up in heaven and a team of angels behind her when needed. Jimmy wondered if he would ever see that side of her in action.

E. B. broke the silence again and said, "Okay, Maura's about to wake up."

Maura stirred, and as she opened her eyes, she realized there was sand everywhere—in her hair, on her face, and all over her body in every crevasse. She grabbed the comforter and pulled it up around her chin, sat up, and looked across the pond.

"Wow" was all she could say softly as she took in the incredible scene in front of her. The sky was a pale pink-purple color as dawn was breaking. And there was a soft, beautiful mist surrounding the pond and hovering over the water. It was surreal, a moment of total serenity. And it made Maura wish she had her camera handy.

She glanced over at Bob to share the moment, but it was clear that he was totally out, with his face planted in the sand. Maura sighed in contentment and smiled as she looked at him and remembered the amazing night they'd had. She went back to staring at the water, and at that moment she could hear the sound of the water lapping gently on the sand. At the entrance area of the pond, she spotted a lone swimmer starting to do laps. She thought he was most likely a long-distance swimmer, one of many that frequented Walden Pond to train for the Olympics.

As she watched him, Maura realized he would be the first of many that would come to the pond in early morning to exercise and train. She knew she and Bob needed to get a move on, especially since the sun would be rising soon. She turned to Bob, and as much as she hated to disturb him, she started to shake him gently awake. He didn't stir. "Odd," Maura murmured. "He's always the early riser." She started to shake him more firmly and said, "Bob, wake up. Come on. We need to get going."

Bob groaned, turned onto his back, and said, "What?"

Maura looked down at him. "Sorry to disturb you, but we have to get moving. It's almost daylight, and people are starting to arrive to swim." He still hadn't opened his eyes. He just murmured, "Oh my head," in response and covered his face with his hands.

Maura could clearly see he was in pain and that he didn't want to open his eyes—not a good sign. She started to get dressed quickly as Bob lay prone on the beach. "Honey," she said. "I'm sorry your head's in pain, and I know the last thing you want to do is move—but we have to! We need to hightail it out of here before a park ranger arrives and tells us we're trespassing, since it's clear we stayed here overnight."

Bob still didn't open his eyes, and he just said, "Yeah, okay, whatever," and didn't move.

Maura stared at him, frustrated, and thought, *Seriously? When did he get so trashed last night?* Then she said, "Okay, here's the deal. I'm going to pull everything together and take it up to the car while you pull your pants and yourself together ASAP."

"Yup" was the reply with still no movement.

"All righty then," Maura said. She let out a loud sigh and started gathering items, except the comforter, which Bob clearly still needed. As she left for the parking lot, she said over her shoulder, "I'll be back in a jiffy, so hopefully you'll get it together by then."

When she arrived back at the pond, Bob was dressed and slowly putting his sneakers on. As Maura watched, she marveled at the reality that she was now finally engaged to this handsome man. It made her burst into a big smile, walk over, throw her arms around him, and say, "I love you!"

He blinked and said, "Yeah—I know," and lightly kissed her.

Looking deep into his eyes, she added, "Thanks for an amazing night. I'll never forget it—*ever*."

Bob grinned slowly and said, "Well, that's good to hear!"

Maura turned toward the water and could see now three colorful swim caps moving out on the water as they swam. "Okay, we've gotta get out of here now. It's almost total daylight." And with that, she started grabbing anything remaining, including the comforter, which she pushed into Bob's arms.

Bob watched her in action, mystified. First of all, he knew she was NEVER awake at that hour in the morning, and second, she seemed very happy with him as well. As much as he tried though, he couldn't remember any details of the night before, except arriving at Walden. The rest was a fuzzy blank blur. *But clearly*, he thought, *it must have been a good time and a great night on the pond.*

Once everything was accounted for, Bob and Maura walked together up the steep entranceway out to the parking lot. As they were climbing up the big hill, a ranger was coming down. Maura held her breathe as Bob said, "Good morning." The ranger gave them a big smile and said, "What a beauty for a sunrise, huh? Can't beat that on Walden Pond" and kept going.

Maura kept trudging up the hill and was happy when they reached the car. She dumped everything in the trunk, and once Bob was buckled in, she started driving back to their meeting spot from the night before. Along the way, she stopped for coffee, since Bob clearly needed it for his hangover. He was quiet the whole time, which Maura thought was odd. But she decided his head must just really hurt. Still, she remembered what an incredible night it had been, and she was surprised he hadn't brought up anything about their engagement or the wedding proposal.

Once they were getting close to their meeting spot, she said, "So, Bob, who do we tell first about our big news?"

He looked blankly at her. "What news?"

Maura laughed and said, "Our engagement, silly!"

Bob sat up straighter in his seat, turned to her, and replied, "What engagement?"

Maura almost went off the wrong exit when she heard his reply. She immediately went pale, and with a stunned expression on her face, she said, "Bob, what are you talking about? We got engaged last night. You proposed to me."

Bob's face turned white. as he said "No, I didn't."

Luckily, at that moment Maura was turning off the highway. There was totally silence as she drove down the road and into the parking lot where his car was. She flew into a parking spot, turned off the engine and stared hard at him in disbelief.

"Are you going to tell me that it was a bad dream, a delusion, or that you don't remember last night?"

Bob gulped and softly said, "I don't remember."

"What?!"

"Look, Maura, you know where I stand on this. I am never remarrying. I made that clear to you a long time ago. Nothing has changed on that viewpoint. And just because I tied one on last night and got overemotional in the moment and proposed doesn't mean that we're now getting married."

"But you said you loved me, and all these other wonderful things," Maura said, choking up and holding back tears.

"I *do* love you. You know that! You're my soulmate in life; there's no one like you. But I like things the way they are. Our relationship works great as is, so let it be."

Maura was speechless and said in a low growl, "Get out of

my car *now*. I don't believe a word you just said for a second, or that you don't remember last night."

Bob looked at her and could see how upset she was. "Look, I—"

She put up her hand and snapped, "*Stop*—just get out."

With that, Bob opened his car door. As he walked away, he turned and said, "For what it's worth, I had a wonderful time"

Maura turned her face away and didn't say a word. She was too choked up to speak, and she didn't want him to see the tears brimming on the edge of her blue eyes. As soon as his got in his car and drove off, she started sobbing.

Jimmy, Pat, and E. B. had traveled in the back of Maura's car from Walden. They heard what Bob had to say, and they were left with a devastated woman in the front seat to deal with. Maura at this point was crying so hard she was starting to hyperventilate.

E. B. spoke first. "I can't believe it. This is *so* not good. Maura is going to spiral out of control in a big way." She turned sideways to look at Jimmy and snapped, "How can he do this to her?"

Jimmy replied in a quiet, concerned voice, "I don't know. I'm truly sorry."

"Well, we need to get this situation under control before she hyperventilates."

Pat piped in. "Well, I think I should follow Bob. Clearly he's suffering from a bad hangover and driving with one as well. So I can catch up and drive with him, and also try to figure out what he's truly thinking and report back."

"Okay, that sounds like a plan," replied E. B.

Pat got out of the car, and once out of view, she spread her beautiful glistening wings, which shimmered the colors of the rainbow, and flew away in search of Bob's car.

Meanwhile Jimmy was sitting in the back of the car in stunned silence, next to E. B. He didn't know which to be more upset about: the stupid bonehead move his brother had made or the emotional mess of a woman in the front seat. Seeing Maura that upset unglued him. Just as he was to turn to E. B. and ask, "What now?" Maura started the car.

E. B. immediately jump up and over to the front passenger's seat. She quickly looked back at Jimmy with concern written all over her face and said, "What the heck does she think she's doing starting the car? She can't see, she's crying so hard! Oh, Jimmy, I told you this was going to spiral and become a bad situation."

For the first time, Jimmy saw the true love she had for Maura and could feel the panic emanating from her. In a different scenario, he might have sat back and enjoyed this moment to see E. B. unraveling—but clearly not then.

Maura backed up the car, drove out of the parking lot, and headed onto the highway going north. E. B. turned again to Jimmy. "There is no way we can stop her from driving. It's her free will, and we can't interfere with that. But how can she drive when she can hardly see?"

"No worries, E. B. I've got this!" Jimmy said as he quickly moved from the back seat to the front driver's seat with Maura. Since he was a spirit guide and couldn't be seen, he was able to slide his angelic body between her and the steering wheel. Jimmy then proceeded to put his hands over hers on the wheel and his feet over hers on the accelerator and brake. He turned to E. B. with a big grin and said, "Hot damn! This works! And I love driving."

E. B. gave a big sigh of relief and relaxed a bit. "Good move, Jimmy. I don't want to imagine what could happen today with her so unfocused and not seeing or thinking clearly."

As they started heading north toward her home, Maura started talking out loud, asking, "Why didn't Bob want to marry me? What is wrong with me? God, why did you put me on this earth to be so unloved? Is it some sort of survival test on earth? Why does that have to happen to me?" She started crying harder again and said, "There is no reason for me to even be here." With that awful statement, she drove by the highway exit for her home.

As she was having this conversation E. B. was distraught. She leaped up from the passenger seat, went to the back seat behind Maura, and wrapped her with as much love and warm energy she could push forward as she enfolded her from behind. "Oh no, no, Maura! You are so wrong. You are *so* loved from above, by so many souls in heaven. We try to pour as much love toward you as needed daily, but sadly you don't always feel it. I love you and protect you always as your main guardian angel. Jenny prays every day for you and shines her incredible light down to keep you safe. And now you even have Jimmy as your new spirit guide. And there is always God, who loves you unconditionally. You must never forget this."

But sadly Maura was so distraught, she wasn't tapped into feeling or sensing E. B. or anything she was saying. She just kept driving north with Jimmy focused on not letting go of the steering wheel.

All of a sudden, E. B. gasped and with a serious look on her face said, "Oh, Jimmy, I think I know where she's going! I hope I'm wrong."

Jimmy was trying to keep his angelic stuff together as he looked back at a very stressed out E. B. *Damn! Never thought I'd see her coming totally unwrapped in front of me. But it just proves how serious the situation is with Maura and how much she meant to E. B.* Having two women losing it in the car was not cool, and he wasn't sure what to say or do.

Just then, he swore he could hear Norm's voice as clear as a bell in his head, saying, "This is why I chose you, Jimmy, to protect Maura. It's your time to shine." In that moment, Jimmy felt a sudden boost of confidence. He turned and said, "E. B., where do you think we're going?"

"To a private beach on the North Shore. It's a favorite spot of Maura's. When she arrives, if she goes the wrong way and takes the seawall entrance down to the beach—oh, I don't know what will happen! The seawall is ancient, narrow, and crumbling from all the damaging storms that have occurred over the years. It's a place with bad steps, and if you hit the wrong step, you could easily fall off the wall. And the worst part is the path is high above the ocean, and under the waves there's nothing but big, sharp rocks. So if you were to fall, you would slam against the rocks and most likely die. I hope that Maura doesn't go this way, because if she were to lose her balance—" E. B. started to get choked up and couldn't finish the sentence.

She finally said, "I hope her emotional state doesn't make her go this route."

"Now, let's not jump to conclusions," Jimmy replied. "She might just be out for a pretty drive to calm her emotions, and maybe she'll stop for some lobster!" He flashed a quick smile her way.

"I don't think so, but let's pray I'm wrong," E. B. said somberly. "Speaking of that, I hope Jenny is up in the prayer room gathering a bunch of angels to pray with her for Maura."

Jimmy looked quickly behind him at Maura, and and stated "Well, it looks like she's calming down, so the prayers must be working."

At that moment, Maura turned off the highway and started following the signs that said "Marblehead." Jimmy felt it was a good time to let her drive on her own, since they were off the highway, so he went to the back seat. He sat and thought about all that had happen in the last few hours. She was in his care now, and nothing his brother had done that morning was going to change that.

As they started to drive along the ocean, Jimmy could visibly see Maura calming down more. He wished he could sing to her but then realized the radio was right there. As he glanced at E. B., who was deep in thought, looking out the window, he said, "Hey, I'm going to turn on the radio now. Let's come up with some cool songs to sing along to and cheer Maura up."

"Excellent idea!" E. B. said, and she focused her energy on having Maura turn on the radio. Jimmy focused on some lively dance tunes, and soon they were coming through as Maura flipped the channels. She started to smile and sing along to some of the music, and what she didn't know was that Jimmy was singing along with her, and E. B. was making some happy dance gestures as well and clapping along to the lively tunes.

As things just seemed to be lightening up, Maura turned down a road with a sign that said, "Welcome to Marblehead." E. B. stopped clapping, got very attentive to where they were going, and held her breath that it was the right direction to the main entrance to the beach. But Maura turned right off the main road to go down a side street where she had lived years ago and parked at the end of it.

E. B. moaned, "Oh no, Jimmy. This is where the seawall entrance is."

Jimmy knew then that what Maura ended up doing in the next few hour was all that mattered. And it was up to him to make sure nothing went wrong. He jumped out of the car when she did and turned to E. B. and quickly said, "Don't worry. Unlike the poker game, I will not take my eyes off her, and I am laser focused on protecting her. It's my job!" With that he walked by Maura's side along the seawall path with E. B. in tow, somberly and intently praying her heart out.

CHAPTER 12

The Seawall

Maura walked down the narrow pathway that led onto the seawall. She stopped and assessed the situation. It was a much narrower path than she remembered, with random breaks in many areas along the wall. It was clearly crumbling. Where there used to be stairs closer to the beach, they had broken off.

She looked way down to the ocean and could see the high tide coming in. Waves where starting to crash up against the wall. It was a beautiful location overall, and Maura stood there and took it all in, breathing in the salty air. Then slowly she walked along the crumbling path carefully and sat down at the highest point in the middle of the seawall. She promptly started to cry her heart out again and repeatedly murmur, "Why?"

No, wait, thought Jimmy as he watched her. *It's a wail from the depths of her soul.* It was gut-wrenching to hear and watch, and he wrapped his angel arms around her to protect her from the edge of the cliff and all the pain she was inflicting on herself. He could feel all her hurt and anguish and would have done anything he could to erase what his brother had caused. *She doesn't deserve this!*

At that moment, E. B. came to Jimmy's side and said, "Oh, Jimmy, what if she jumps? If she does, she will hit the sharp edged rocks below and die on impact."

Jimmy didn't reply at first. He was too concerned, because he knew she was right, and from E. B.'s energy, he could feel her stress and immense worry. Then E. B. said quickly, "Jimmy, listen. We need to come up with a plan. And we need to act fast! The top priority is that you need to save her if she jumps."

"Oh sure, E. B. How's that supposed to happen? I don't have wings." Jimmy snapped.

"Well, you can leap down and jump up to catch her if she falls. You're her spirit guide, and that's now your job, Jimmy," E. B. said firmly.

"OK ... and pray tell what will you be doing?"

"Exactly that—praying hard and asking for a miracle."

"Really? Well, that's good stuff, E. B."

"Look this is serious, Jimmy. If she dies, the person who needs to release her soul to heaven is me. I don't want to have to do that! But that's my job; it's what I do." And with that E. B. turned away, because she was starting to get choked up.

"Well, that's not going to happen—not on my watch," Jimmy said firmly. "I don't want you ever to have do that until it's her time. So you go say your prayers, and I'm going to practice leaping from the edge of the seawall to the water until I can do it at MOC 5 speed!" He turned his attention back to Maura just as she edged her butt closer to the edge of the cliff.

He never took his eyes off her as he practiced his drill. It reminded him of being back in the army, leaping down, landing on a rock to make sure he could catch Maura, and then jumping back up onto the seawall. Jimmy did this until he found a perfect rhythm and path that would make his movement as fast as possible to catch Maura, if she jumped.

Maura currently just sat at the edge, despondent and forlorn with red puffy eyes.

Right at that moment, Norm appeared from the other side of the seawall and made his way quickly to E. B. She gasped and said, "Oh, Norm, thank goodness you're here! I was praying for a miracle, and now you're here to help! Maura is in a bad way."

"I clearly can see that."

"What can we do?"

"I'm not sure, but we need to snap her out of this despair state quickly before she does something that we will all regret." With that he approached Jimmy on the middle of the seawall.

"Norm!" Jimmy said as he leaped up from the ocean to the top of the seawall.

"Pretty impressive stuff, Jimmy. Good job! I need you to come with me and brainstorm with E. B. on what we can do to help Maura." Jimmy stopped practicing and walked over to Norm and E. B.

Norm said, "Let's quickly review Maura's life when she was in a bad place and it was a close call. Any thoughts?"

"What about the time Lad, her dog, saved her when she was a teenager?" E. B. said.

"Good thought, but it's too obvious if we bring him into this situation. Lad's been gone a long time, and it would seem a unbelievable coincidence. She would think her mind was playing tricks on her."

"Well, clearly Maura loves animals," Jimmy stated. "And it would cheer her up to see one. Wait! What about the bulldog, umm, Ugly, that brought Bob and Maura together. Remember? It was the second time they met."

"Yes—he's right!" said E. B. "Ugly would be perfect! Though I can't believe they named him that."

"True, that was definitely an intervention," Norm murmured. He thought about it for a minute and then walked back over to where Maura was. He knelt in front of her, looked into her puffy eyes, and said, "How is it you don't know how deeply you are loved—every day by all of us above? I'm so sorry about Bob and the situation. I am going to do everything I can to help fix it, but we need to help mend you, your heart, and your soul first—and fast." With this he wrapped her in a warm, loving white light.

Maura looked up to the sun and felt the warmth invade her being. She had no idea it was Norm, next to her, sending as much love as he could. She then went back to staring at the waves, mesmerized. The high tide was still coming in, and the waves were getting higher and crashing powerfully right near were Maura was sitting. Seeing this, she started to untie her sneakers and took them off.

Norm observed this action and stated "Okay, this is getting serious. I'll be back shortly." He walked toward the end of the seawall, toward the pathway. He then quickly turned back and said, "Jimmy, keep practicing the drill to catch Maura if needed."

"And E. B., just keep being you."

To this E. B. replied, "I don't want to take her to Heaven, Norm! Please don't make me be the one to do it."

"I know, E. B. Let's hope and pray you don't have to." And with that Norm quickly dashed away toward the entrance area of the seawall.

Once out of sight, Norm morphed into a hawk and flew high up in the sky, extended his huge wings and gliding slowly. His piercing eyes were focused on the side streets below in Marblehead, and with each block he flew further away from the seawall and Maura. Finally he saw what he was looking for and quickly dove down and landed softly on a large branch of a pine tree.

At that moment, Winston the bulldog was desperately starring out the kitchen screen door toward the lawn. He needed to go out something fierce, but his owner was preoccupied upstairs or just not listening. Winston barked loudly one more time, and with no response, he murmured to himself, "Screw it," stepped back, and rushed forward. He leaped through the screen door, ripping it apart. When he landed on the grass, Winston sighed loudly in relief.

And then he heard, "Hello, Winston," not from inside the screen door but above him. He looked up fast and realized he'd know that voice anywhere. Incredulous, he said, "Boss? Whatcha doin' here? What's wrong? I know I just busted in a screen door, but I hope you're not here because of that. Things must be really slow in Heaven, if you are!"

Norm chuckled and said, "No, Winston, but I do need your help today."

"Anything. Norm, you know that."

"Okay, so I need you to run like the wind as fast as those short legs will take you to the seawall about four blocks away. You know where it is, right?"

"Sure, Norm, but I'm not as young as I use to be and a much chubbier bulldog too. Maybe I can catch a ride on your hawk wings?"

"No, Winston. You can do this if you put your mind to it. I'll be right above you to guide you along."

"Okay then, I'm off! But tell me while I'm running my big butt off—why am I doing this?"

Above him, Norm flew along and filled him in. "There's a woman on the seawall, Maura, who's considering jumping off the cliff, because she's very distraught. I need you to distract her. You are going to remind her of a different bulldog, and hopefully it will make her rethink falling off the cliff and get her in a better mood overall. She loves dogs. Bottom line, Winston, you're going to have to pour on the charm and love for Maura."

"Got it, Norm," Winston replied, panting heavily as he ran.

"By the way, she's going to call you by a different name. Please just go with it, okay?"

"I'll do my best, as always," Winston puffed out slowly in reply.

"I know, and please hurry."

Back at the seawall, Jimmy stopped practicing. He knew what to do now to perfection. He decided it was better to stay at Maura's side and watch her and hope she didn't make a stupid move.

Maura continued to stare at the rising tide, totally mesmerized by the crashing waves. She was looking very forlorn as she sat there.

At that moment, Jimmy looked up into the sky, and he couldn't believe his eyes. Hovering over Maura and around E. B. were hundreds of angels as far as he could see. It was the most amazing sight he had ever seen. All of them illuminated tons of light and love down on Maura and around E. B. It was beyond overwhelming and brought tears to Jimmy's eyes. As he gazed up at this incredible sight, in the center of the mass of angels he saw Jenny with the most immense light of all shining down.

In that moment, Jimmy knew THIS was where he now belonged and his purpose in heaven. He turned to E. B. in stunned silence and awe.

E. B. smiled slowly and said, "Welcome to the miracles of heaven, Jimmy. The army of angels are always around us and at my command when I need them. I asked them to come down today to surround Maura with as much love as possible, in the hope that she feels it."

Jimmy jumped down in front of Maura again and

exclaimed, "Maura, I SO wish you could see the hundreds of angels surrounding you!"

Suddenly Maura looked up and seemed to stare right at him. At that moment, Winston came barreling around the corner of the seawall entrance.

"Wait," Norm said loudly. Winston immediately sat down gladly. He was panting with his tongue hanging out of the side of his mouth.

Norm, still circling above, said, "Catch your breath. Calm down. I don't want you showing up ready to drool all over her!"

"Ohhh boy, do I need to cut back on the doggie biscuits!" Winston said in between big breaths.

"Okay, Winston, trot slowly over to Maura as if it's just another day on the seawall. But stop just before you get to her, and sit up against the wall itself. In order to pat you, she'll need to come away from the cliff's ledge."

"Got it, boss." Winston proceeded to move slowly down the path toward Maura.

Norm flew high above and watched to see if miracles would unfold.

When Winston was almost to the center of the seawall, Maura turned her head, gazed away from the water, and spotted him. She stared wide-eyed with her mouth hanging open as Winston inched closer.

Winston didn't have a tail, but it didn't matter. He started wiggling his hips and butt like crazy as he got closer. He stopped about ten feet from her and sat down against the seawall. There he waited to see what Maura would do. Then he put his paw up in the air as if batting at something, hoping she'd reach back and grab it.

Maura just sat there stunned, not moving. Soon she said softly, "Ugly! Is that you? It can't be."

Winston barked loudly, looked up at the sky, and said, "You're kidding me, right? We might be a bit of a homely breed overall, but I am one of the more distinguished-looking ones." Holding his head up high, Winston looked up at Norm and said, "Look at this face—not just a mother could love it!" With that he focused back on Maura and raised his paw in the air toward her.

Maura was transfixed. She couldn't believe she was looking at the same dog that had brought Bob and her together so many years before. He was an English bulldog with no collar or ID, a stray that followed them around. And so they called him Ugly affectionately. And now, on a day that she was so upset over Bob, after all those years, out of nowhere an English bulldog had appeared again.

Winston wiggled his butt and stretched out toward her just enough so that Maura would have to lean back to pat him. And it worked; she started to shift her body away from the edge of the cliff and slowly reached back toward him. Winston made sure he was back up against the seawall, pulled his head and paw back, and waited.

Maura inched closer to him and started patting his head and said "Oh, Ugly, I've had such a bad day, but seeing you here has to be a sign from above." She reached out to cradle his paw, and with that Winston leaped up and started smothering her face with sloppy kisses. He knew she needed that more than anything.

Jimmy jumped up and exclaimed, "E. B., look! She's moved away from the cliff's edge! Yes!" E. B. smiled and clapped. And in response, angels from above starting singing. Jenny stayed in the middle and kept sending light and love from her celestial being.

But Winston knew his job wasn't done yet. So while Maura thought he was playing with her, he started gently tugging at her jacket until he had inched her closer to the wall and further from the cliff edge. At that moment, Winston spotted her sneakers, and he knew what he had to do.

He lay down and turned over on his back, so his stomach was exposed, and looked up at Maura. She laughed and started to rub his belly. At that moment, Winston pulled a ninja move. He rolled back over in the other direction, leaped to his feet, grabbed one of her sneakers in his mouth, and started backing away from her and the seawall, moving toward the entrance path.

Maura couldn't believe how fast he had moved and that her sneaker was in his slobbering mouth. "Ugly, wait! That's my sneaker. I need it!"

Winston kept backing up with his eyes glued to her, whispering to himself, "Come on, come on." He started wiggling his butt again.

In an instant, Maura jumped up and started walking away from the edge of the seawall and toward Winston, and the path. He quickly kept moving backward, and once she was solidly on the path and close to the entrance, he dropped the sneaker.

From high above, and circling the situation, Norm said, "Excellent work, Winston!"

Winston, still playing with Maura and wiggling his butt off, barked, "I'm expecting a *big* doghouse made of dog biscuits when I get up there, Norm. A mansion-size doghouse!"

Norm laughed and said, "Done, Winston!"

Meanwhile, E. B. was jumping up and down in happiness to see Maura out of danger, and Jimmy was standing there in disbelief that he didn't have to save Maura and that he got upstaged by a dog. Damn ... And as his thoughts started to drift to "What's next?"

At the entrance to the seawall, a sandy-blond, middle-aged, tanned man appeared, shouting, "Winston!"

Winston whipped his head around and thought, *Uh oh, I not only ripped the screen door, I also ran away.* So he turned, sat back down with his "sad face" look, and waited for his owner. When his owner reached him, he looked down and said, "Winston, there you are! What are you doing on the seawall of all places?" Then he glanced over and saw Maura, and said, "Did you find my dog?"

"Ummm, no. To be honest, he found me," Maura said as she began putting her sneakers on.

"Huh, well, gotta say it's really strange behavior from him. He busted through a screen door and ran away. He *never* does that. I was really concerned."

Maura looked up and said, "I'm really sorry. He just showed up on the seawall a short time ago. But he reminds me of another bulldog I knew years ago, so I'm really happy he made an appearance—even though he stole my sneaker!" Maura smiled and then laughed. That laugh reverberating off the cliff wall was music to Jimmy, E. B., and Norm's ears.

Maura then stood up and observed the handsome man in front of her as he put out his hand and said, "Hi, I'm Cameron." She smiled back and introduced herself.

Winston observed below and barked his own commentary. Cameron looked down and firmly said, "Okay, that's enough from you today, Winston! I think you've caused enough drama and excitement for one afternoon."

Maura quickly jumped in. "He's an amazing dog, and I love his name!"

Cameron laughed. "I named him after Winston Churchill because of his face."

"I can see a bit of the resemblance," Maura replied. "And like Winston Churchill, your dog is a hero. I'm so glad I've met him, today especially."

Cameron studied her for a moment and said, "So, what brings you to the seawall today?"

Maura looked back out over the rough water and crashing waves against the seawall. "Oh, I just came here to put my feet over the ledge and have the waves kiss my toes as the high tide came in."

Jimmy, who was observing this interaction from the opposite side of the path, whipped his head around to look at E. B. "She's kidding, right?" he asked.

Seeing his stunned reaction, she said, "Of course! She doesn't want some stranger to know the truth of where things were heading ten minutes ago."

Cameron said, "Well, I'm going to head back to my friend's beach house that I'm renting with Winston."

And Maura responded, "I'm going to my car on the side street."

Together they walked out of the entrance of the seawall path, with Winston happily in tow. When they got out to the street, Cameron turned and said, "It was nice meeting you, Maura. I hope you got what you needed today from the seawall and the waves."

"Yes, I did—and Winston, believe it or not, was a big part of it." As they approached her car, she turned and said, "You know what I realized while I sat on the edge of the cliff today?"

"What?"

"That every day God sends you love and miracles and messages. And it's up to you to see, hear, and accept them."

Winston barked in agreement.

Cameron looked down at him and back at Maura with a smile. "Well, it seems that works for Winston." Then he looked at her seriously and said, "That's the nicest thing I've heard said in a long time. Thanks for sharing that."

"You're welcome," Maura said quickly and then crouched down to hug Winston and say good-bye to him. "Thanks for showing up today, buddy," she whispered in his ear. With that, she got into her car, and Cameron waved and shouted, "Safe travels." She waved back and drove away.

As she got onto the main road in Marblehead, Maura sighed. She started to boot up her cell phone, which she had left in her car, and thought, *What a crazy emotional day this has been ... BUT I'm still here.*

And at that moment, an alert came through on her cell phone that Bob had called twice but left no message. Maura stared at the phone and said out loud, "Whatever. I can't deal with anything else today." She turned the tunes on and drove toward home.

Meanwhile, as Cameron and Winston walked back to the beach house, Winston looked up at the sky and barked, "Thanks, boss, for the adventure."

Cameron looked down at him and said, "Honestly, Winston, what is *up* with you today?" If Winston could talk he would have said, "Look up—that's the whole point!"

Norm, still sailing high above them, said to Winston, "You are the rock star of the day. Thanks for the miracle. I promise you will get your biscuits." And with that, he flew out of sight, toward the opposite side of the seawall.

As Norm reappeared to Jimmy and E. B., they were all smiles and excitement.

"Norm, that was a great idea we all had," Jimmy stated happily. "It worked, and Maura's on her way home, and alive."

"Great job protecting her, Jimmy. You really showed me how far you've come in the short time since you've been in heaven."

"Great, Norm! Hey! Doesn't this mean I won the Roman

coins? And we can all play poker again?" Jimmy quickly replied with a hopefully look on his face.

Norm chuckled and said, "Ahhh, Jimmy, I'll work on getting the poker games reopened for everyone."

E. B. murmured, "Thank the Lord for that."

Jimmy smirked. "Game on, E. B.!" He then looked serious and said, "Wait! What about my brother?"

"Pat's coming to get you and will fill you in on the latest," Norm replied.

With that, Jimmy started to walk toward the entrance so Pat could connect with him there. As E. B. watched him go, she turned back to Norm and stated with a smile, "Another day, another miracle for us."

Norm replied, "Not 1 miracle, but 2 happened today, and that's why I showed up." With E. B. looking at him quizzically, he smiled and said, "Let's go home!"

As they both looked up, there was Jenny smiling down on them. Using all her celestial energy she created an exquisite staircase made of crystals and light for Norm and E. B. to climb up on and head back to heaven.

Then said Jesus unto him, Except ye see signs, and wonders, ye will not believe.

—John 4:48

EPILOGUE

Two Months Later

Maura was lying in bed, totally exhausted. It was time to get up and get ready for work, but she had already hit the snooze three times. "What is wrong with me?" she mumbled.

It seemed that every other day she was dragging around with no energy. Even more annoying was it seemed she was developing a sensitive stomach. Randomly she would feel sick.

Over the weekend, Maura thought she had the flu, so she had laid low, tried to eat better than normal, and gotten a lot of sleep. She had hoped that had done the trick, but now it was Wednesday, and she didn't feel good again.

Maura sighed, pushed herself out of bed, and got ready to start the day. But as soon as she went to brush her teeth, she immediately turned toward the toilet and threw up. She sat down on the floor, weak from the experience, and said to herself, "Again?"

And that's when she froze. Everything stopped, including her breathing, as a thought clicked in her head. "Every morning!" Maura gasped. As the reality of that statement sunk in, she started shouting, "No, no, no, *no!*" She promptly ended up vomiting again from the reality of the situation.

She finally got up and reached for a washcloth, poured cold water on it, and promptly put it on her forehead. Sitting back down on the bathroom marble floor, in the silence she could hear her heart thumping loudly in her chest.

Maura hadn't heard from, talked to, or seen Bob since the infamous day on the pond and the seawall. She had decided not to talk to him until he left her a voicemail explaining where things stood, and see if he had a change of heart. She never thought she'd go that long without talking to him, and she felt lost without his presence in her life. He hadn't called even once, and she was blown away by that.

What Maura didn't know was that Bob had called her twice while she was on the seawall, and when she didn't answer, he felt that was a message back to him that she wanted nothing further to do with him—as hard as that was to comprehend. Bob sadly acknowledged that he had lost his favorite girl—and soulmate— for all the wrong reasons. He walked around in a stunned daze most of the time and had gone on more than one bender to help dull the pain. Pat was constantly at his side, trying to give him signs of guidance—but he wasn't sensing them.

Maura sat there alone on the marble floor, and wondered, *How am I going to tell Bob?* She stared into space, then closed her eyes and rocked back and forth.

ACKNOWLEDGMENTS

Life is like a tapestry of intertwining events, encounters, and serendipity. I believe it's all orchestrated from Heaven as part of each soul's path and intentions on earth. Based on this personal belief, I am writing these acknowledgments to show how this book came to be over time.

About ten years ago, I was in Vegas, celebrating a birthday with friends. One of my best friends gave me a gift certificate to the hotel spa. It was for a relaxing massage, and I couldn't wait to chill out.

I ended up with a young woman who seemed a bit nervous, but was sweet and kind. Unfortunately it didn't start off right; she ended up dripping oil over my third eye, and the oil ended up almost going into my eyes, my hair, and all over my face. But I took some deep breaths and tried to relax. She continued but kept staring at me and saying she thought I reminded her of someone. She swore we had met, but I said, "No, that hasn't happened. I never come to Vegas."

At the end of the spa session, as I was about to get up, she exclaimed excitedly, "I know who you are! You're an earth angel!" She proceeded to tell me she had been at an angel seminar the weekend before, and because of that class, she knew how to identify me.

I was thinking, *What?* but instead I laughed, said, "Thanks for letting me know," and I bolted out of the room in search of my friends.

When my friends heard the story, they almost fell off their barstools laughing. And for the rest of the trip, I was constantly introduced as "the earth angel." Who knew that was the beginning of a long, strange, but wonderful trip to enlightenment?

My friend Christine was so amused by that whole encounter that she kept the joke going after I got home, and she bought me a subscription to *Angels on Earth* that Christmas. Who publishes that quarterly booklet? *Guideposts.* Thus was the beginning of my journey with angels—stories, encounters, and even hearing them.

Five years later, while in Maine for a getaway weekend, I picked up a pen and started writing this book. I can honestly tell you I didn't stop, couldn't stop, till my hand hurt so much I had to finally put the pen down. By then, I had written five chapters.

I will always feel then and now that I was spiritually guided to write this book. I didn't know about automatic writing at the time, but I can reflect back and tell you this is what it felt like. The thoughts, the words, the characters, and the images were urgently waiting to be put down on paper.

There are SO many wonderful people and places that helped make this book happen.

Like Tim, a seasoned poker player who took the time out of his day job as bartender at the local Cuban restaurant to guide and teach me about the ins and outs of serious poker tournaments. Tim, without your knowledge, I never would have been able to write about the Poker Game. Thanks so much!

To the incredible spirit artist Rita, who drew a picture of Jimmy, when I went to her and said, "I can't stop hearing this man's voice in my head!" Thank you for making me realize I was not losing my mind. Rita was also a key part of my spiritual development over time. Most importantly, her encouragement and feedback helped me finish this story.

Thanks also to Karen Paolino, for her incredible Angel Knowledge, and the amazing classes at Heaven on Earth.

Though there were many interruptions in finishing this book over the years because of life's demands, the following people never lost faith in my ability to tell this story, so it could be shared with others. They pushed me forward constantly with their encouragement and love of the book:

My number-one fan from the day she read the first first chapter, Gina you are such an inspiration. I can't thank you enough for all your love and encouragement.

To my top readers, supporters, and editors along the way: Christine, Maryanne, Alan and Isadora, Cathi, Michael, Michelle, Jayne, and Gretchen. There were so many others that said, "Keep writing," including my Mom. Thank you!

To all the incredible places I was given access to, which were such an inspiration for my writing: Walden Pond; Cape Elizabeth Island, Maine; Kennebunkport, Maine; Manomet Beach, Plymouth; The Beach House, Plymouth; Preston Beach, Marblehead; and Lincoln, MA.

A *huge* thank-you to Guideposts publishing for embracing my story and wanting to publish it.

And finally—and most importantly—to all my angels, spirit guides, Jimmy, and most importantly to God for giving me this gift to write what I hear.

Please note: If I missed anyone above, I didn't intend to. I am grateful for all your support.

Printed in the United States
By Bookmasters

$11.99   08/11/17

LONGWOOD PUBLIC LIBRARY
800 Middle Country Road
Middle Island, NY 11953
(631) 924-6400
longwoodlibrary.org

LIBRARY HOURS

Monday-Friday	9:30 a.m. - 9:00 p.m.
Saturday	9:30 a.m. - 5:00 p.m.
Sunday (Sept-June)	1:00 p.m. - 5:00 p.m.